VALENTINE'S TRAVELS

They sat side by side atop the coachman's bench.

"I think of you as 'Mistress Mischief,' for obvious reasons," said Cole.

Marcie bowed her head, quickly hiding the shimmer of tears that suddenly sprang to her eyes. Only one other person had ever called her Mistress Mischief.

"I have offended you," said Cole, misunderstanding her reaction.

Marcie blinked away the wetness from her eyes. She looked up at him. "Quite the opposite. You see, my father used to call me Mistress Mischief."

"It seems I am forever stirring up memories for you."

"Yes," she whispered. "It does seem that way, doesn't it?" And as she spoke, she felt a tiny tremor of feeling inside her breast, a feeling she could not quite express. Happiness at the memory of her father? Yes, it was that . . . and yet it was so much more complicated, and had more to do with the man seated beside her.

Cole Coachman reached over with one gloved hand to pull up her carriage rug. "Wouldn't want you to catch your death," he murmured.

His gloved hand brushed against her own, and Marcie felt a shiver tingle up her spine. Of a sudden, she could not help but notice how very near he was. She could smell the crisp, clean scent of him, and the delicious smell of cedar emanating from his greatcoat and red scarf. The world sped past as the coach whisked over the road, and to Marcie it seemed as if there was only just herself, Cole Coachman, and Prinny the owl alive in the universe. What a very cozy place it was . . .

ZEBRA'S REGENCY ROMANCES
DAZZLE AND DELIGHT

A BEGUILING INTRIGUE   (4441, $3.99)
by Olivia Sumner
Pretty as a picture Justine Riggs cared nothing for propriety. She dressed as a boy, sat on her horse like a jockey, and pondered the stars like a scientist. But when she tried to best the handsome Quenton Fletcher, Marquess of Devon, by proving that she was the better equestrian, he would try to prove Justine's antics were pure folly. The game he had in mind was seduction—never imagining that he might lose his heart in the process!

AN INCONVENIENT ENGAGEMENT   (4442, $3.99)
by Joy Reed
Rebecca Wentworth was furious when she saw her betrothed waltzing with another. So she decides to make him jealous by flirting with the handsomest man at the ball, John Collinwood, Earl of Stanford. The "wicked" nobleman knew exactly what the enticing miss was up to—and he was only too happy to play along. But as Rebecca gazed into his magnificent eyes, her errant fiancé was soon utterly forgotten!

SCANDAL'S LADY   (4472, $3.99)
by Mary Kingsley
Cassandra was shocked to learn that the new Earl of Lynton was her childhood friend, Nicholas St. John. After years at sea and mixed feelings Nicholas had come home to take the family title. And although Cassandra knew her place as a governess, she could not help the thrill that went through her each time he was near. Nicholas was pleased to find that his old friend Cassandra was his new next door neighbor, but after being near her, he wondered if mere friendship would be enough . . .

HIS LORDSHIP'S REWARD   (4473, $3.99)
by Carola Dunn
As the daughter of a seasoned soldier, Fanny Ingram was accustomed to the vagaries of military life and cared not a whit about matters of rank and social standing. So she certainly never foresaw her *tendre* for handsome Viscount Roworth of Kent with whom she was forced to share lodgings, while he carried out his clandestine activities on behalf of the British Army. And though good sense told Roworth to keep his distance, he couldn't stop from taking Fanny in his arms for a kiss that made all hearts equal!

Available wherever paperbacks are sold, or order direct from the Publisher. Send cover price plus 50¢ per copy for mailing and handling to Penguin USA, P.O. Box 999, c/o Dept. 17109, Bergenfield, NJ 07621. Residents of New York and Tennessee must include sales tax. DO NOT SEND CASH.

Miss Marcie's Mischief
Lindsay Randall

ZEBRA BOOKS
KENSINGTON PUBLISHING CORP.

ZEBRA BOOKS are published by

Kensington Publishing Corp.
850 Third Avenue
New York, NY 10022

First Printing: January, 1995

Printed in the United States of America

To Randy and Jason, who are my own forever valentines. And to the following special people who helped move us into the future: My incomparable in-laws, Robert "Andy" and Betty Anderson, for their generous hearts; my brother-in-law and his wife, Bob and Becky Anderson, for the many good times; Dave Keesler, who took special care with my hard drive and modem; my sister and her husband, Debbie and Larry Tanner, who always leave a light lit for me; my niece, Sheri, whose smile and true heart will forever make me happy; my nephew, Larry, who is a supreme gentleman and a true hero-in-the-making; my brother, Bill, and his fiancé, Jody, who've found their own special road; my father, William Coleman, who makes me feel safe no matter what route I choose; and G.G. and Aunt Bert, who can wreath any journey of mine in warm hues.

And to Jane Leakey and Rita Scanlan, who continue to be wonderful hosts, beautiful people, treasured friends.

Author's Note

England's storied past has long held a lure for me, and the Regency period—that short span of time between 1811 and 1820, when George IV was sworn in as Regent and later ascended the throne as King of England—is one that will always enchant me. I am intrigued by the meticulous manners of those who peopled this time, of their grace and wit, their stirring pride and sense of honor, the zest with which they set out upon the open road, and most especially their eccentrics. It is this eccentricity and interest in travel that truly holds my fascination.

My characters and their adventures to the Cotswolds are purely fiction, of course, and any Regency aficionado will realize I have indeed taken some artistic license in the telling of this tale. For instance, I allowed the dashing Marquis of Sherringham, a member of the Whip Driving Club, to take the reins of a mail coach. In actuality, members of the various driving clubs at this time would imitate the dress and manners of stagecoach drivers, and not mail coach drivers. Transporting the Royal Mails was a serious and exacting affair; townsfolk often set their clocks with the arrival and departure of the these coaches, and the Post Office demanded the utmost punctuality on the road. And certainly none of these brave drivers lingered overly long at their various stops as the marquis and his passengers do in my tale, nor did they take on extra passengers or parcels not listed on the coach's way-bill, as the marquis so generously does.

However, in this "great age of coaching," I decided my story would be best suited if the handsome hero settled his sights on driving a Royal Mail coach and not a mere stagecoach. After all, the Marquis of Sherringham is a punctual and exacting fellow—until he meets the heroine, that is! And what better place for a romance to occur than aboard a Royal Mail coach brimming with bundled confections, letters penned to loved ones, and packages wrapped in hearts and flowers that must reach their destination before the close of Cupid's special day?

I'd like to believe that this tale of a spirited, mischievous miss yearning for freedom, for *love*—and her titled, handsome swell who, too, itches to be free to love and live as he chooses—could have taken place, and aboard a Royal Mail coach, to boot. If not, it should have.

So I invite you, dear reader, to join me and my characters as they set off on a madcap journey to the Cotswolds, a journey that is bound for love, and for a Saint Valentine's Day that holds magic and promise and all things wondrous . . .

Here's hoping the mail brings something special to you this Saint Valentine's Day.

Lindsay Randall

One

It was the eve of Saint Valentine's Day, and Miss Marcelon Victoria Darlington was feeling far lonelier than she'd ever felt in her life. Valentine's Day was a day for lovers. A day for dreaming and dancing and being pleasantly pierced by one of Cupid's arrows. It was a day when little else counted except for that one special other person.

Unfortunately, Marcie had no "special other," no potential suitor with whom she could look forward to a day of merrymaking, a day for hiding a lacy heart made by her own hands and intended for her chosen gentleman to find.

There would not be a posy of flowers left on her doorstep by an admirer, no loving Valentine verse, and certainly no waltzing within a man's warm embrace at a Valentine's Day ball for Marcie.

She stood alone amid a wintry world, one void of any shining knight who might bring pink-blossomed daphne to press into her hands. Saint Valentine's Day might as well be a world away from her, Marcie thought miserably.

Though late of St. Ives and much accustomed to the cold and the wet, Marcie found herself in high fidgets as she stood shivering in the snowfall and awaiting her ride out of London Town. She was, after all, running away from boarding school. The fact that her hired carriage was dreadfully late did not sit well with the eager-to-be-gone Miss Marcie.

"Hell and damnation," Marcie muttered to no one but herself. Depressed, and saddened by the approaching day intended for love and lovers, she drew her fur-lined pelisse more closely about her and swore soundly as though she'd had not a whit of schooling under the stern Betina Cheltenham.

Marcie stared grimly out from the snowy mews near Mistress Cheltenham's School for Young Ladies and verily cursed her luck. By all accounts, she should have been far away from the City by now . . . and far away from the switch-wielding Mistress Cheltenham.

But here she stood, watching from the shadows as a lone vagabond wove a zigzagging path through the piling snow to stare in stupored wonder into windows festooned with beribboned hearts on the inside and frosted with swirls of ice outside. Somewhere, a church clock struck the quarter, then the half hour. Where the devil was the conveyance her good friend Nan Farthington had promised would come?

Marcie didn't fear the high-and-mighty Mistress Cheltenham's sense of outrage should the old bat discover Marcie's plot to be free; she feared the woman's switch! Marcie had had the back of her hands stung by Mistress Cheltenham's switch too many times to count. The last flick of that horrible stick had been because Marcie had not properly executed the precise procedure in eating an artichoke.

Artichokes. What a perfectly senseless waste of time in even bothering with them. Marcie hated artichokes perhaps more than she despised Mistress Cheltenham's rule. Marcie had suffered the old hen's horridness only because traveling to London and enrolling in Mistress Cheltenham's School for Young Ladies had been the final request of Marcie's dear beloved father, Argamont, who in keeping with his wild reputation, had snapped his foolish but lovable neck at a rasper while riding the hounds. He'd just celebrated his sixtieth birthday—and Marcie her seventeenth—on the day Argamont Darlington decided he could still ride with the best of the young horsemen. Too bad for Argamont that he'd chosen the most spirited of horses.

Marcie's grief at her father's passing knew no bounds, and surely it had been profound sadness that propelled her to do precisely as her father had wished. She'd dutifully come to London and unpacked her trunks in Betina Cheltenham's drafty attic room, determined to mold herself into the fine lady her father had longed for her to become.

But life within Mistress Cheltenham's crumbling walls was surely a fate worse than death. Marcie's spoilt school mates looked down their prettily upturned noses at her, viewing her as naught but a wild West Country girl who would never achieve the genteel manners necessary to catching the interest of a fine man. As for Betina Cheltenham, the woman had immediately tried to crush Marcie's inherent sense of adventure and fun. Mistress Cheltenham and Marcie locked horns from the moment they'd met.

Betina preferred teaching the daughters of those Cits who weren't as wild and unreigned as Argamont, Marcie's father, had been. Betina preferred her charges to be like porcelain dolls, and she'd gotten her wish. All of Mistress Cheltenham's students, save Marcie, had been fashioned to be helpless, pretty, and as far as Marcie was concerned, proved to be oftentimes deucedly temperamental.

Marcelon Victoria Darlington, however, was neither spoilt nor demanding. She was her own person, and she was as lively as the day was long.

For Marcie, the supreme idea of fleeing the boarding school to the safety of her godmama's home in the north had seemed a simple and very smart thing to do only a few hours past. But that had been before the snow began coming down in heavy, pristine flakes that chilled to the bone. Not even Marcie's ermine tippet could keep her fingers warm now.

All her other schoolmates had been whisked away from the school by loving family members who promised their cherished daughters sweet Valentine buns to eat, time enough to carve hearts from paper and embellish them with lace and verses and, no doubt, expensive bottles of perfume with which to scent those same hearts. There would be late-night banquets for her schoolmates to enjoy, and dancing until the wee hours of the morning.

For Marcie, though, there would be too little merriment this Saint Valentine's Day. Dear Argamont was dead, leaving only his vast monetary holdings in his wake. Marcie's mother had died in childbirth when Marcie was but five years old. She had no siblings. All the family left to her were two girl cousins—the lovely Meredith and the independent Mirabella—both of whom had written to Marcie begging her to join them for Saint Valentine's Day in the Cotswolds, and both of whom she hadn't seen in years.

It seemed her Darlington cousins had now found Marcie the perfect parti in the form of some boring Marquis of Sherringham. It was paramount, they'd written, that Marcie come join them for the holiday so that both Meredith and Mirabella could help school the younger Marcie in the fine art of capturing his lordship's interest. *They,* too, intended to transform her into a lady.

In a pig's eye, thought Marcie. She was naught but the willful youngest Darlington cousin, with a wealth of riotous red hair and a spirit more prone to riding with the wind than suffering a moment of unease in any gentleman's presence.

Her father, Argamont, after a colossal argument with his brothers, had abruptly cut himself off from the Darlington family. Though he and his two brothers, Percy and Manningford, had pooled their collective geniuses and created a wildly successful financial industry known about London Town and across Europe and beyond as the Darlington Three, the men had been too prickly ever to work together for long.

Once Argamont had amassed a staggering fortune, one vast enough and steep enough to see that Marcie as well as several generations beyond her need never want for a thing, he'd severed his ties with the Darlington Three. He'd then whisked a young Marcie off to the extremities of Cornwall where he indulged them both in fresh air and restless seas. Argamont had never truly wanted to spend every waking hour worrying over money. Though he'd been thrilled by the challenge of creating something from nothing with his brothers, once the future was secured, he chose to spend his time enjoying life to the fullest.

While Marcie's cousins had learned to dance and be witty, Marcie had been set free on the rugged coasts of Cornwall, unfettered by any reins. Surely Mirabella and Meredith didn't realize what a challenge they faced in trying to reform Marcie.

At last, horn blaring, a conveyance came careening down the snowy lane.

Good Lord, Marcie thought to herself, that loud horn would wake the dead—not to mention the crotchety Mistress Cheltenham! Leave it to Nan to come for her with a telltale clatter of noise.

Marcie grabbed her worn portmanteau and scurried out of her hiding spot, intent on waving down the driver and encouraging him to quiet his loud horn. She gave not a whit of thought for her own safety as she ran pell-mell out of the mews. Her only thoughts were to quiet the incessantly

blaring horn, and then to board the conveyance and be forever gone from Mistress Cheltenham's stuffy school. With
the promise of sweet freedom only a few steps away, Marcie
ran straight into the path of the oncoming carriage.

"Hell and damnation!" Cole swore loudly as he steered
the spirited tits—three chestnuts and a bay—deucedly close
to the body of a caper-witted female bent on destruction.
He reined in sharply. The horses reared dangerously, then
ground to a halt on the snow-covered lane, barely missing
the wench by inches. Lucky he didn't break the fool chit's
neck—or worse, one of his trusty horses' legs.

"Are you all right?" Cole demanded, watching the girl's
wide-eyed face through a gust of snow spitting up from the
horses' hooves.

"Oh, quite fine," she called back, rallying herself mag-
nificently. "Now if you would please settle those beasts I
will be but a minute climbing in the carriage."

Cole wondered if he'd heard her aright. Didn't the female
realize he was running a mail coach out of London to the
Cotswolds? The Royal Mail stopped for no one and for
nothing! Dash it all, but her caper was going to set him
behind time.

Cole strained to make out her slight form amidst the
heavily falling snow as she bent to retrieve something from
the middle of the lane. Being a gentleman, Cole had no
choice but to secure the reins, drop down off the bench and
go to her aid.

"You ought to take more care when crossing the street
at such an hour and in such foul weather." He spied the
article she sought and quickly lifted the ugly portmanteau

she'd dropped during the confusion. "Good lord, it's heavy. What have you got in it? The family jewels?"

"Heavens, no." Her prettily-sculpted features took on a look of absolute dread as she mistook Cole's attempt at humor quite seriously. "My eldest cousin was bequeathed all of the jewels my father had purchased over the years. And to my middle cousin went most of the lands my father acquired during his lifetime."

"And you?" asked Cole, not expecting a plausible answer. Though a moment ago he'd been annoyed by the female's presence, he now found himself unwillingly interested by this mere slip of a girl who'd scampered out of the snowy mews and talked as though she were a miss of means with great wealth in her family tree. She intrigued him not only with her foolish bravery of waving down his coach, her outrageous talk of acquired lands and jewels, but also with her stunning good looks.

"Fossils," she answered, craning her neck to view the carriage behind him. Absently, she added, "Lots and lots of fossils. I never was much interested in precious gems or gold, and as for land, I don't believe it should be owned by only one person but should be shared with all of God's creatures." She nodded toward her bag. "I've my best fossils in the bag you hold, you know. I intend to give them as Saint Valentine's Day gifts. I say," she said, frowning when she realized both the fore and hind boots of the carriage were crammed with parcels and hampers, "do you think my portmanteau will fit beneath that large box lashed to the hind boot? I do hope so, for I fear there is no other place for it."

She immediately took the bag from his gloved hands, giving him a nod of thanks for retrieving it, then headed for the back of the carriage, clearly intending to strap the thing in place on her own. She called a cheery "Hallo!" to

John Reeve, the stone-faced guard who clung to the conveyance near the hind boot, and whose sole duty it was to
protect the letter mails. Surprisingly enough, the usually
dour Reeve actually cracked a smile at the female!

What the devil? Cole wondered.

"Now see here," he called out. Cole forced himself to
forget her pretty features and even the fact that he'd nearly
run her down. "I have a schedule to keep, and keep it I
will. I haven't the time to take on any extra parcels. And
more importantly, neither you nor your parcels are listed on
my way-bill. This is a mail coach, mistress!"

"But I'll only take a minute—"

"A minute I haven't got," he grumbled. "You'd best find
yourself a stage coach in the morning."

"But morning will be too late! Oh, dash it all," she muttered, looking forlornly at the coach festooned with wild
game and barrels of wine, all destined for the snowy north
of a Valentine's Day England. "Can you not find a place for
me within the carriage? I'll sit on boxes. I'll hold my own
baggage upon my lap. Why, I'll even hold several bags!"

Just then, there came the sharp sound of a woman's oily,
high-pitched voice. "Marcelon Victoria Darlington, if you're
out here, you'd best show yourself!"

A buxom woman, heaving mightily, her face pinched,
came wheezing out of the mews. She wielded a sturdy
switch which she slapped forcefully against one large thigh.

"I am warning you, Marcelon!" Slap! went the switch,
cutting through the crisp night air. "You don't want me to
lock you in your attic room again, now do you?" Slap!
"What a pity it will be for you to have nothing but bread
and water, and be alone on Saint Valentine's Day." Slap . . .
slap . . . slap!

The pixie-faced girl turned wide, emerald-green eyes on Cole.

"Oh, please," she whispered. "Do you have room for me or not? My good friend Nan promised me you would. She said—"

"Nan? Nan Farthington?"

"None other."

Devil take it. Cole should have known his illegitimate— and decidedly rambunctious—half sister Nan, now perched within the coach and looking forward to her journey into the Cotswolds aboard a fast vehicle, would promise a convenient escape for a runaway minx!

He wondered if Nan had also mentioned that Cole was in fact the Marquis of Sherringham and had arranged this coach drive in keeping with his membership duties in the Whip Driving Club.

Lord, he hoped not. His lordship was looking forward to a rousing drive through the North country, and he rather liked the idea of teaming through the lanes in the guise of Cole Coachman.

"Well, then, do climb in the carriage," ordered Cole, unwilling to disappoint his half sister. God knew Nan had been dealt a harsh blow in life due to the fact she'd been born on the wrong side of the sheets. Cole had long tried to make some amends toward her.

He quickly moved to prop open the door and deposit the girl into the mass of bandboxes, Valentine hearts, and ribbons inside. He helped stuff her oversized portmanteau in after her. She would have to take it upon herself to find a place to perch in the crammed quarters.

Cole slammed the door shut, then made a quick leg for the bench. He'd no sooner scooped up the reins and clicked his fine beasts into motion than the overweight woman came tottering round the mounting block, switch in hand and a very unladylike curse on her overly reddened lips.

Cole tipped his broad-brimmed low-crowned hat in her direction as his horses shot forward. Within moments, he was riding hard for the north. He could only imagine what he'd gotten himself into by helping one Marcelon Victoria Darlington in her queer dash for freedom. He reminded himself to give Nan a good dressing down. Until then, though, he had a schedule to keep, wayward runaway on-board the coach or not.

Marcie, thrown off balance by the jolt of the coach, slapped her palms against the ceiling of the crowded interior, and soundly cursed both the switch-wielding Mistress Cheltenham and the fact that her friend Nan had obviously not fore-warned the coachman of her plan to board his conveyance.

"I know you're here somewhere, Nan," said Marcie into the darkness of the coach. "You might as well present yourself."

Nan Farthington, stifling a yawn, propped her head up between a pile of bandboxes and pink ribbons that had spilled free of a package.

"Marcie? Is that you?"

"Of course it is me, you ninny! Who else would so fool-ishly step into the path of an oncoming coach? Really, Nan, when you said you'd come for me in a coach before mid-night, I'd thought you meant a hired conveyance and cer-tainly not a Royal Mail coach!"

Nan, wiping the sleep from her eyes, giggled when she spied a tousled Marcie looming above her and holding on for dear life.

"I fail to see the humor in all of this," said Marcie.

Nan's grin widened. "You look a fright, Marcie, not at all like the heiress you truly are."

Marcie frowned. "I don't suppose you realize I was nearly knocked senseless by that team of spirited horses rigged to this coach, nor that Mistress High-and-Mighty nearly caught me in the act of fleeing."

"I guess I fell asleep," said Nan, looking guilty, but only for a moment. "Here," she said, "have a bonbon. They tumbled out of a poorly-wrapped package during a most dangerous turn a few blocks back."

"You're eating someone's Valentine's treat!"

"Well, you didn't expect me to just let them roll around on the floor, now did you?"

No, Marcie thought, of course she didn't, and she had to smile. Nan Farthington had been the delight of Marcie's dreary stay in London. She'd met the girl not at the odious school but rather during one of her many larks of slipping away from Miss Cheltenham's iron-fisted rule, and exploring Town on her own. Marcie and Nan had literally stumbled into one another at one of the many book fairs held within the inner city.

They'd both been dashing for the same book, a collection of romantic poems. It hadn't taken Marcie but a moment to become friends with the talkative Nan. The two young women decided to pool their coins, purchase the book, and share it. They'd taken turns reading passages to each other, giggling, and then reading some more. Over the next several weeks, they became thick as thieves, sharing secrets, and dreams, and more than a few adventures.

Marcie had been surprised to learn that Nan was an illegitimate daughter of a peer of the realm, a man Nan chose not to name. Marcie might have felt sorry for the young girl for being born out of wedlock, but Nan's was a lighthearted spirit, one that didn't encourage sympathy. Indeed, the girl seemed to do quite well for herself, free to dash about Town whenever and wherever she chose. Clearly, someone connected to Nan's mysterious father saw to it Nan and her mother were comfortably housed and nicely clothed.

Nan obviously wanted for nothing and, in truth, seemed to enjoy her unfettered freedom. She'd brought a ray of bright sunlight into Marcie's long, dark winter in London. Marcie was glad she'd become such close friends with Nan, and wondered for the hundredth time, at least, how she ever would have endured the past bleak months if not for the chatty and fun-loving Nan Farthington.

Nan popped another confection in her mouth, chewing happily. "You'd best find a place to prop yourself, Marcie. Cole takes every turn as though the hounds of hell are nipping at his heels," she said, pulling Marcie's thoughts back to the present.

Just then, Marcie was thrown into a pile of boxes as the coachman, true to Nan's words, whipped round a corner.

"Heavens!" Marcie cried. "I shouldn't be fretting about Mistress Cheltenham's switch but should be worrying whether or not I'll make it out of the City alive."

Nan giggled again, obviously enjoying their madcap race through the snowy streets. "I've never known you to be such a worrier, Marcie."

" 'Tis only because I've never had the misfortune to ride in a coach driven by—what did you say his name is?"

"Along the road, he is known as Cole Coachman."

"And off the road?" asked Marcie, fearing the answer.

Nan's eyes twinkled. "Oh, many things, I daresay. But we shall call him Cole Coachman. He is adored along the road. Why, all the ostlers and innkeepers make a race to rush to his bidding."

"Marvelous," muttered Marcie, finally finding a place to sit between the bandboxes. "I've a demon for a driver who is considered a veritable god along the road. Well, so be it. Just as long as he takes me safely to the inn at Burford."

"Burford! I thought you were heading for Stow and your godmama's estate. Didn't you say your cousins have found you a perfect match in some fine swell?"

"That was the plan, yes. But now that I am free of that horrid boarding school, I've decided I am not so inclined to make his lordship's acquaintance. I rather like my freedom, Nan."

"Fiddlesticks! What girl doesn't dream of being married to a marquis?"

"This girl," said Marcie. She sighed, relaxing at last. "Truly, Nan, I do not fashion being forced into marriage—and certainly not with some boring Marquis of Sherringham."

"Mayhap he is not as boring as you think," offered Nan.

Marcie leaned back against a box, sighing again. "Oh, I am certain he is a total bore—from the top of his head all the way to the tips of his champagne-polished boots. My father swore that all swells were full of themselves and boring to boot."

Nan grinned mischievously. "Ah, well, we've miles to go before you meet your Marquis of Sherringham. Did I happen to mention I am heading to my mother's uncle's house in Stow to spend Saint Valentine's Day in the country?"

"No," said Marcie, wondering exactly *when* Nan had decided to make the trip. No doubt when Marcie had begged her friend to help devise an escape route from Mistress Cheltenham's school. How like Nan to want to be in the thick of things. In any event, Marcie was relieved to hear her friend would be joining her on her way to the Cotswolds.

"We'll have a grand time, Marcie. Trust me," said Nan with a wink. "Now, I want you to relax. Let us enjoy our adventure, shall we? Cole Coachman always has the best of fun on his madcap coach ride. I am certain you will find his presence anything but boring."

Marcie had her reservations as she thought of Cole Coachman, fenced in his huge winter coats, with a lone hothouse rose adorning one buttonhole and that low-crowned hat slanted over one gray eye. He'd seemed to her impatient and haughty.

But as Cole Coachman directed his finely trained team through the narrow city streets with frightening precision, Marcie couldn't help but feel a sense of safety.

Too, she was feeling a smug satisfaction at having outwitted the switch-wielding Betina Cheltenham. Her night's escapade had been a success after all. Things were indeed looking up.

"Pass the bonbons, will you, Nan?" Marcie said.

Nan didn't have to be asked twice.

Two

The Marquis of Sherringham found himself quite exhilarated by the blinding snowstorm he met just two miles north of London Town. Nothing like a strapping ride aboard a Mail coach, he told himself, highly pleased with his decision to neglect—for Saint Valentine's Day, at least—his many duties in pursuit of grand adventure. His two sisters-in-law and their demanding brood of girl-children were forever in need of something from him.

Even now their voices echoed in his ears: "Sherry, can you not spare a few more pounds for a new gown for Penny? She has naught but rags to wear this Season! I swear she'll swoon should she be forced to wear such threads!" This after Cole had seen to it the gawky Penny had been swathed in the blush of fashion by none other than the finest modiste of London. And then there was always the chatter of his nieces with which to contend. "Uncle Sherry!" they'd carol in unison upon sight of him, "Mama promised you'd take me out and buy me some lemon ice. Well, yes, today! When else?" And, "Of course a ride along Pall Mall! You didn't think Mama would have me be seen riding anywhere but, did you? Oh, but we'll surely expire if you don't fashion to take us for a ride this very minute!"

Always Cole had given into the many demands. He'd found his coffers heavily depleted and his patience sorely tested by his family. It took every ounce of the gentleman within him not to toss the lot of them out of his home.

Now, though, with a bitter wind slicing through his teeth and catching at the long red woolen scarf he'd bundled about his neck, he blessedly felt a world away from his London home and all the matters his title heaped upon his heart.

What a veritable pleasure it was to utilize all of his strength in keeping the spanking team in line and guide them on a sure path through the heavily falling snow. Gad, but he loved the excitement of it all! Nothing but the wind and the snow and his own wits in dealing with the fine horseflesh before him.

Cole released a satisfied sigh, squinting his gray eyes against the slanting snow and watching as his breath made perfect spirals in the cold air. For the first time in a very long time, the Marquis of Sherringham—known along the road as the famous Cole Coachman—felt as though he and he alone was master of his fate. Heady stuff, to be sure.

He was in the midst of guiding his hearty team round a very tricky bend in the road when there suddenly came the shattering of icicles and the sound of the coach window being lowered.

Cole chanced a quick glance over one shoulder, seeing the poke of Nan's ridiculous bonnet and then the full of her cherub's face. As always, her mouth was opened.

Nan was screaming like a banshee, but the wind blasted her words away. Cole could make out nothing more than something about bonbons, Betina, Burford . . . and dying.

Dying?

"Say what?" Cole shot back, quite unsettled.

The Mail guard, John Reeve, clinging for dear life to a strap at the hind boot—for he'd decided to use his bench for the two huge hat boxes he was transporting north to a very special female—shrugged his shoulders, looking as perplexed as Cole felt.

Nan, meanwhile, forced her plump body halfway out the window.

"Stop!" she shouted into the spitting snow.

Cole pulled too hard on the reins, making the lead horse rear against his suddenly harsh hand and causing the others to shy to the side. He muttered a curse as he finally got the beasts under control and managed to lead them to the side of the road—what he imagined was the side of the road, anyway. The snow was dangerously deep.

The coach no sooner came to a stop than the door banged open and the red-haired chit he'd saved from the snowy mews came bounding out. She didn't even need a step to help her alight. She executed a perfect jump down into the snow as though she'd spent a lifetime climbing in and out of trees. She ran a few paces into the deep snow, then stopped, swaying ominously.

"Oh!" exclaimed the plump Nan, now at the door of the coach. "She's going to faint, I swear. *Do* something, Cole!"

Cole had no choice but to leave the box. Within a moment, he was at the girl's side, the snow covering the tops of his boots, filtering down into his hose. He studiously ignored the chilling wetness and forced himself to forget that he was losing precious time on his Mail run.

"G—go away," the girl gasped.

"I can hardly do such a thing. Looks to me as if you could use a helping hand. Besides, Nan's been muttering some such thing about Burford, Betina and—what was it?— oh, yes, bonbons."

The girl slapped one gloved hand over her mouth. "Oh," she groaned, "did you have to mention b—bonbons?"

"What about bonbons?"

Cole had his answer just as the red-haired minx turned away and deposited the contents of her stomach atop the pristine snow. That done, she neatly collapsed at his feet.

Marcie awoke to the sounds of Nan's clucking and Cole Coachman's curses. Both were hovering over her. Since the man's voice sounded so dreadfully angry, Marcie decided it best to pretend to be unconscious.

"Poor thing," Nan fussed, "she's been locked into an attic and given nothing but bread and water for weeks!"

"And why was that? Is she a thief, Nan?"

"Lordy, no! Least I don't think so. No, I'm certain she isn't," added Nan a second later. "She would have told me if she were. We've shared all kinds of secrets. I can tell you she's spirited, though."

"And long overdue for a proper meal," observed Cole.

His statement made Marcie inwardly wince. She hadn't thought she'd become *that* thin. As for Nan's theatrical cry of Marcie's having naught to eat but bread and water for weeks, well that just wasn't true—though, of course, Mistress Cheltenham had *tried* banishing Marcie to her room with only bread and water. But Marcie, inventive as she was mischievous, consistently outwitted the old hen. Indeed, she'd made handy use of a rope pulley the maids often used for the hanging of laundry. With just a few hearty yanks— and several coins paid to the son of the baker who lived next door to the boarding school—Marcie had enjoyed a veritable feast in her drafty attic room each night, until Mistress Cheltenham had discovered what was afoot. She'd cut down the rope only a week ago, and since then Marcie had been forced to dine on whatever she could pilfer from the kitchens when Betina Cheltenham wasn't looking.

Nan sighed dramatically. "I should have known better than to share a box of confections with her. Whatever shall we do, Cole? Take her back to London? I fear she might never come round! Do you think she'll live?"

Marcie took that moment to flutter her eyelashes. She caught sight of the man named Cole. He was peering straight at her. His eyes were the color of London at dawn, all misty and gray and quite ominous. Oh dear, thought Marcie, clearly seeing the man would like nothing better than to yank her to her feet and rattle her soundly.

Marcie quickly pressed her eyes shut tight.

"I think she'll survive," said Cole, obviously wise to her feigned state of unconsciousness. He got to his feet.

Nan continued to pat Marcie's wrists. "Still," she lamented, "you should take more care when charging along the road, Cole! Not everyone is accustomed to your fast pace."

"Then not everyone should so eagerly climb aboard my coach. Especially not runaway thieves."

At that, Marcie snapped her eyes open. "I am no thief!" she sputtered.

The coachman turned a sharp eye toward her. "I thought that might rouse you."

Marcie felt her pale face grow hot. Blast him, she thought, he'd tricked her!

"I—I am no thief," she said again. "As for being a runaway, I am barely that. I have every right to travel where I wish, when I wish."

"And your wish, I take it, was to steal a ride on my coach."

"Nan told me you are headed for the inn at Burford. So, too, am I. Trust me when I say I intend to pay you for your trouble, sir."

The man cocked one dark brow at her. "I'll be taking no stolen coin, and certainly none from any runaway."

"Now see here," Marcie cried. She brushed away Nan's assistance and got to her feet, squarely facing the broad-shouldered coachman. "I tell you once and for all that I am no thief! As for that prison of a boarding school from which I dashed, I had every right to come and go as I pleased. Do you hear? Every right indeed."

"I hear you quite clearly," replied the tall coachman, "as must all of God's earth. Really, miss, but must you shout so?"

Marcie hadn't thought she was shouting—but then again, the ringing in her ears near drowned out everything but her own queerly beating heart.

"Oh, no," she muttered.

She was going to faint again. She'd been so caught up in indignation that she'd given not a whit of thought to her earlier queasiness. Of a sudden, she saw the telltale pinpoints of light flashing at the back of her eyelids. The ringing in her ears grew louder. She felt her body grow hot. In another moment, she'd doubtless find herself face first in the snow.

"I—I fear I am going to be sick again," she whispered.

Nan gasped, jumping out of Marcie's way.

Cole Coachman, however, neatly stepped behind Marcie, took a gentle but firm grip on her shoulders, and then eased himself and Marcie down onto a snow-covered bank. His muscled legs straddled her while the ends of his greatcoat made a blanket beneath her.

"Lower your head," he instructed into the shell of her right ear. "That's it. Now breathe. No, not like that," he whispered when Marcie breathed too fast and too shallowly. "Like this."

Marcie listened to the even, deep sounds of his breath swooshing into her ear. She followed his lead, doing exactly as he instructed.

"Ah, you are a quick learner. Very good. Now, I want you to close your eyes," he said, his voice husky and reassuring. "Close your eyes and think of the crisp, country air filling your senses. . . ."

The ringing in Marcie's ears ceased. By degrees, she felt herself calming. Gone was the queasiness that had so quickly surfaced.

Cole Coachman obviously sensed her ease. To Nan, he said, "Go to the coach and get my pack from the box. There's some ginger root there. Fetch it for me, will you, Nan?" As Nan hurried away to do Cole's bidding, he returned his attention to Marcie.

"Feeling better?" he asked. "No, don't get up, and don't open your eyes. Not yet. Just nod if you're feeling better."

Marcie stayed where she was. She nodded.

The clean, musky scent of the man traveled up her nostrils, enveloping her in a warm and wondrous cocoon. She found herself resting ever so gently against the lean length of him. Feeling no need to be on her manners lest the man move away and she become violently sick again, Marcie allowed herself a moment of pure pleasure in just remaining within his sturdy embrace, no matter how indecent it might be to do so.

Said the handsome coachman, "I fear someone should have warned you about Nan and her penchant for devouring an unholy amount of sweets. She seems to have a stomach made of stone in that respect."

Marcie shook her head. "I fear I am the one to blame. I should have known better than to eat so many confections."

"And I," said Cole Coachman, "should have taken more care when rounding the bends along this winding road. Though it is my duty to deliver the parcels of this coach, I should have given more thought to you and Nan."

Marcie thought him sweet to say such a thing, but his words also reminded her that she was hindering his Mail run.

"I dareswear I've quite made a mess of your schedule," she said.

"I won't argue that point."

Marcie lifted her lashes, turning her face to meet his look. "Do you think you will be able to make up the time I've caused you to lose?"

"Rest assured, I will certainly try. Barring, of course, any quick turns along the road that might cause you to be ill again."

"Please," said Marcie, chagrined. "I am quite over being sick for the night. I feel right as rain. Truly, I do."

"Glad I am of that."

He grinned then; a handsome grin that tugged at the corners of his chiseled mouth and chased away the clouds in those gray eyes she'd heretofore found so stormy.

Perhaps the man wasn't so beastly as she'd first thought him to be. . . .

Nan came trudging through the snow then, carrying a small square of folded linen. Cole Coachman took the pack from her hands. He made quick work of unfolding the linen and offering to Marcie what looked to be a chip of hard candy.

"It is ginger root," he assured her. "It will help settle your stomach. Now be a good miss and open your mouth."

Marcie did as he instructed, all the while keeping her gaze locked with his. She felt the smoothness of his gloved fingers as he placed the chip of ginger root between her lips, then brushed those same fingers across her cheek and down her jawline. All thoughts of ever again being sick quickly fled. Heavens, but she found herself quite mesmerized by the man's touch, his nearness, his grin.

Ginger root or not, she was feeling much better. Quite alive, in fact. And far too aware of the man's presence.

"Think you can stand up now?" asked Cole Coachman.

His question forced Marcie out of her trancelike state. Blast! she thought, but she was acting like some moon-eyed schoolgirl. What a ninnyhammer she was being to think that the coachman's haunting grin might be a prelude to some sort of courtship. As Nan had stated, Cole Coachman had many admirers . . . and perhaps several lovers as well. As for Marcie, though she was an heiress in her own right, she remained at heart a wild West Country girl, innocent of the ways of roguish coachmen who kept a mistress at every post. For Marcie to fashion any romantic notions out of this bizarre meeting was nothing but pure folly. Marcie chewed on the ginger root even as she pulled away from the man's heated embrace and got to her feet.

"I am quite ready to continue our travels," she announced, "that is, if you are not averse to my joining you."

Marcie fully expected the coachman to inform her he would deposit her at the nearest inn, all else be damned.

Thank goodness, he did no such thing.

Instead, he stood up, brushed the snow from his coat, then gave her a grin—one that instantly dazzled her. "My team awaits," he said, indicating the coach and its horses with one sweep of his right arm.

Marcie couldn't help but smile. For the first time since her father's death, all seemed right in the world. She lifted her skirts and headed for the coach, all the while thinking her madcap dash from Mistress Cheltenham's School for Young Ladies was indeed shaping up to be nothing short of a smashing success. How easy it had been!

Marcie was feeling quite pleased with herself as Cole

Coachman moved beside her to help her alight into the carriage.

Of a sudden, though, there came to her ears a terrible screech of fast-moving wheels. She looked up to behold a private carriage rounding the bend—and heading straight for their stilled coach.

"Lord have mercy!" screeched a wide-eyed Nan.

"God save us!" added the guard, Reeve.

"Oh, bloody hell," muttered Cole Coachman.

He expertly grabbed for Marcie, yanking her out of harm's way. But Marcie, sensing danger, had already commenced to jump back. The two of them crashed into each other, the combined momentum of their movements throwing them off balance.

Marcie found herself tumbling backward in the snow, Cole Coachman beneath her. There came the horrid sounds of horses nickering in fright and carriage wheels screeching to a halt on the icy roadway as Marcie and Cole Coachman hit solid ground and began to roll.

"Oof!"

Marcie wasn't certain if that sound came from Cole Coachman's lips, or her own. No doubt from both of them, she surmised, for they tumbled against a stout tree trunk, Cole hitting first, and Marcie following to land with a thump against his solid form.

"Oh, heavens!" Marcie said, trying to disentangle her limbs from his. "I *am* sorry. You are not hurt, are you?"

Her skirts were woefully tangled with his legs. And her left hand was pressing against a part of his anatomy no lady would ever in her right mind even fantasize about! Marcie felt her face redden as she struggled frantically to be free.

Cole Coachman swore in exasperation. "Just stay still, will you?" he demanded.

Marcie, however, was far too embarrassed to stay put. She jumped up, backed against the tree, and in doing so managed to jar a clump of snow from the branches above. The clump came down with a *kerplop* atop Cole Coachman's head, causing him to look like a half finished snowman.

Unfortunately for Marcie, she found she had a hysterical desire to giggle.

Cole Coachman said nothing for a full minute; time enough for Marcie to discern the stormy orbs of his eyes amidst all that wet, clinging snow.

Oh, my, she thought, but she'd be fortunate if the man didn't see her strung by her toes before the night was finished!

Marcie, her urge to giggle sufficiently suppressed, immediately dropped to her knees and tried to brush the snow from him.

"Really, sir," she said in a most serious tone, "but you should have known better than to roll us into this tree."

He glared at her through a fringe of snow. "I can only pray you will forgive me," he managed through gritted teeth.

"Well of course I shall, but—"

Marcie's words stuck in her throat as she glanced up to spy a wedding-cake of a carriage listing dangerously to the opposite side of the roadway and implanted firmly in a snow bank there. The driver, obviously uninjured, was hopping mad and spouting a stream of expletives. He demanded to know what caused a Mail coach to be stopped in the middle of such an oft-used roadway, then screamed for a meeting with the coachman of the carriage.

"Oh, dear," whispered Marcie to Cole Coachman. "I fear the man wants your head upon a platter."

"My head?" sputtered Cole Coachman. *"My head?"*

Marcie blinked and sat back on her heels.

"Well, yes, yours," she said, quite perplexed at his quick-silver moods. "You did, after all, leave your carriage in a most inconvenient spot."

Why the man let forth a clearly long-held breath of frustration, Marcie could not fathom. Cole Coachman, she surmised, could be deuced temperamental!

Three

Cole Coachman righted himself, then peered at Marcie intently. "You are all right, aren't you?" he all but barked at her. "No broken bones? No scraped knees?"

"Only my pride has been wounded," Marcie answered, noting the anger in his wintry gaze.

In truth, his knee had slammed against her ankle during their tumble and Marcie feared she would have quite a goose egg on it before too long. But she would rather walk barefoot on a bed of nails than admit this to the angry Cole Coachman. She'd done quite enough damage for one night.

In any event, he was turning away from her and heading for the livid driver. The two met in the middle of the road, whereupon they engaged in a heated conversation for several minutes.

Marcie moved toward Nan and John Reeve.

"This is all my fault," she said.

No one bothered to argue that point.

Marcie swallowed her embarrassment, then continued, "I see no reason why Cole Coachman should be forced to have his ears bent by yonder driver when, in fact, it was my stupidity that brought us to this unfortunate incident."

"Don't you worry about Cole Coachman, mistress," said John Reeve. "He can hold his own, he can, with any driver along these roads."

Nan nodded in agreement.

"Still," Marcie replied, "he should not be expected to take a scolding on my account."

With that, Marcie headed for Cole Coachman and the sputtering driver. The expletives that streamed from the portly man's mouth were enough to make Marcie's ears burn.

"How very rude!" Marcie admonished.

Both Cole Coachman and the driver turned to gape at her; the pot-bellied driver with a look of murderous intent, Cole Coachman with barely concealed agitation.

"I have things well in hand," said Cole Coachman.

Marcie chose to ignore his warning, instead fixing her sights on the disheveled driver who could doubtless turn the air blue with his broad knowledge of gutter talk.

"You sir," she said, "have no right whatsoever to speak to this fine coachman in such a crude fashion. I take total responsibility for this most unfortunate accident. I am the reason Cole Coachman stopped his coach so suddenly. And it is because of me that he ignored his precious cargo and tarried too long near this dangerous turn."

The gap-toothed driver tipped back his broad-brimmed hat even as he spat a stream of tobacco juice down onto the snowy road. He eyed her but good.

"So she be the one, eh, mate?" he demanded.

"The one and only," said Cole Coachman.

Cole Coachman spoke the words through gritted teeth, Marcie noted, but why he should do so was quite beyond her. She'd only come to his aid, after all. There was no need for him to be so stiff-lipped, nor for him to peer at her as though he wished she were in any other country but the one in which he stood. Heavens, but the man was temperamental; fussing over her welfare one minute, then chilling her with his gray and piercing gaze the next. There was no accounting for some people's moods! she thought.

Marcie straightened her shoulders, focusing her attention on the problem at hand, and on the ugly-voiced driver standing before her.

"Do rest assured that I have every intention of compensating you for any and all repairs to your carriage," she announced.

"Is that right," said the driver, his eyes narrowing.

"That is exactly right," replied Marcie, clicking off the name and address of her sterling solicitor on Holywell Street in London.

The driver guffawed.

Cole Coachman muttered something Marcie couldn't quite make out.

"What!" she hotly demanded, even as Cole Coachman took her by the arm and led her a step or two away from the driver. "I see nothing humorous in my solicitor's name and address. What is all this fuss about?"

"Pipe down, will you?" Cole Coachman demanded. "And for once and for all, cease prattling on as though you are some miss of means with more gold than you know what to do with."

"But I am!" sputtered Marcie.

"Ha," rejoined the driver, obviously listening in on their private chat. "And I be the next King of England." He laughed at his own joke.

Marcie glared around Cole Coachman's muscled bulk, staring daggers at the rotund and very obnoxious driver.

"What an impertinent little man he is," she said.

"And what a spinner of tales you are," Cole Coachman muttered. "Are you mad to make such promises? Why, he'll hunt you down—and the next generation of your family as well—if indeed you do not make good on your ridiculous promise of compensation."

"But I *shall* repay him," Marcie insisted. "And rest assured I have the means to do so. I am the daughter of—"

Marcie never got a chance to finish her sentence.

Suddenly, the door of the toppled coach banged open and a woman, garbed in watered silks and bundled against the cold in a stunning, fox fur carriage rug she'd wrapped about her shoulders, stood framed in the portal of the oddly pitched coach. Her hair was golden-hued and tumbled down in comely ringlets to rest in a tousled mass against the folds of her velvet pelisse. Her eyes were cobalt blue, her pouty lips red as sun-kissed cherries.

"Harry!" screeched she. "Have you left me for dead, you dim-witted fool?"

The fat little driver stiffened in obvious fear. "Good gawd," he squeaked, eyes round and filled with dread. "I done forgot Miss Deirdre!"

He jammed a finger between his lips, digging out an alarming amount of tobacco, flicked the wad to the ground, then spun round to face his beautiful but very indignant mistress.

Marcie might have laughed at the comical sight but for the fact that Cole Coachman was staring with rapt attention at the stunning lady perched precariously in the doorway of the near-overturned coach.

"You might close your mouth," Marcie suggested to Cole Coachman.

He obviously hadn't heard a word she'd said. Indeed, he seemed to have forgotten her presence entirely.

Marcie frowned.

There came a flurry of excitement from the portly driver as he bustled toward the lady, took great pains to help her light, then even stooped to brush the clinging snow from her hems. Marcie wondered why the man didn't also drop to his knees and pay homage to his golden goddess.

"Harry, you little idiot," chided the woman. "Why ever did you leave me to bump my head and then wonder if indeed I'd died and gone to h—"

The woman stopped sputtering the moment she laid eyes on the form of Cole Coachman. Suddenly, her screeching turned to a purr.

"Why, Harry, my *good* driver, how very remiss of you not to inform me we've tumbled across such a handsome gentleman."

Harry tugged at the collar of his too-tight coat. "He ain't no gentleman," Harry spat. "He be the driver of that there Mail coach. And his missus be the reason I ran yer coach into the bank, Miss Deirdre."

Marcie fully expected Miss Deirdre to turn on both Cole Coachman and herself with talons bared. But the wily lady did no such thing. Instead, she gave Cole Coachman a melting smile, all the while ignoring Marcie.

"My good man," purred Miss Deirdre, moving toward Cole Coachman with an obviously affected gait filled with feminine wiles. "You must forgive my driver for his slow reactions. We did not startle you, I hope. And I can only pray we did not do you, nor your horses or cargo, any harm."

Marcie found herself becoming physically ill again as Cole Coachman nearly turned to so much mash in his fine boots.

Oh, for the love of God, thought Marcie. The woman was obviously nothing more than a skilled strumpet. Why in the blazes didn't Cole Coachman recognize that fact?

Marcie fumed as she watched Cole Coachman bend over the woman's outstretched hand, then place a beseeching kiss atop her fine-gloved fingers. A lock of his dark hair tumbled down across his handsome brow as he righted himself and gave the woman a heartfelt smile.

The woman blushed.

Cole Coachman preened.

Marcie wanted to gag.

The next few moments were near impossible for Marcie to bear as Cole Coachman made a complete cake of himself, profusely apologizing to the lady, offering her any assistance he could, and even going so far as to stating he would whisk her not to the nearest inn, but to her appointed destination.

Too bad for Marcie that the lady's destination was none other than the inn at Burford.

Marcie found herself left forlornly alone in the middle of the road as Miss Deirdre tucked her gloved hand into the crook of Cole Coachman's arm and allowed him to lead her to his Mail coach. The lady then ordered her portly driver to remain with her "beloved horses" while she, in Cole Coachman's very capable hands, traveled onward to the nearest inn, at which point help would be alerted and sent to the driver's aid. There remained only the monumental task of transferring the lady's needed luggage onto the coach.

And what a mountain of luggage it proved to be! Even John Reeve was pressed into service by the suddenly mooneyed Cole Coachman.

Marcie felt a moment's pique, watching as the two men restrapped wine barrels, rearranged game and bandboxes in order to make way for the lady's excessive need for space. They certainly hadn't gone to such fuss when confronted earlier with Marcie's single portmanteau!

To Marcie's further dismay, Miss Deirdre took up an entire seat within the coach for herself, leaving Nan crowded against the opposite squabs, and leaving Marcie with no seat at all.

Marcie gnashed her teeth, deciding she'd rather walk to Burford than be forced to inquire if Miss Deirdre would deign to scoot over an inch or two to make room for her.

Nan, comfortably squashed between hat boxes and having, to her obvious glee, found a box of sweetmeats with which to content her ravenous appetite, frowned when she spied Marcie peering into the coach.

"La, Marcie, but I dareswear there is not a bit of extra room in here," she said between mouthfuls. "Mayhap you could ride on the hind boot with Reeve. Or better still, on the bench with Cole. You always told me how you adored riding into the wind while in the West Country. Just think, you could have your fill of wind this night!"

Miss Deirdre, lounging against the squabs in all her silks and furs, cast a cursory glance in Marcie's direction.

"You are a West Country girl?" asked she. "How quaint. And how marvelous that you will find the snow and wind to your liking. I, for one, would near *perish* should I be forced to endure this foul weather for overly long."

Marcie deduced the overly scented she-wolf would no doubt perish should she get so much as a toe chilled.

Nan passed the lady some sweetmeats. "I've some bonbons, too, if you like."

"Bonbons? Oh, how I *adore* bonbons!"

Marcie felt her stomach turn topsy-turvy. There was absolutely no way she would climb into the coach and suffer the sight—or smell—of sweetmeats, let alone bonbons.

"I shall ride on the hind boot," Marcie announced, willing to brave the elements. Anything would be preferable to spending time in a confined space with bonbons and the too-pampered Miss Deirdre.

Marcie closed the door of the coach. With her head held high, she headed for the hind boot.

"What the deuce are you doing now?" demanded Cole Coachman.

Marcie spun round, quite surprised to find the man trailing her. She had assumed he'd forgotten her presence in all the activity.

"I am merely finding a place to roost on this stuffed coach of yours," she told him.

"Then why the devil don't you climb inside and find a seat?"

Marcie blinked at his harsh tone.

"I'll thank you not to speak to me in such a fashion," she snapped back.

"And I," ground out Cole Coachman, clearly itching to be on his way, though the good Lord—and Marcie—knew he'd tarried far too long in his task of indulging the too-beautiful Miss Deirdre, "would thank you to get to the point."

Marcie suppressed the very unladylike urge to kick him in the shin.

"There is no room left for me in the coach," she replied. "Nan and Miss Deirdre seem to have taken up all available space."

"Poppycock. Surely, there is somewhere for you to sit." He made a motion to pop open the door.

"No!" Marcie said emphatically. "There is no need for you to peer into the coach." And no need, she thought, for me to have to witness as you become unmolded clay beneath the very skilled gaze of Miss Deirdre.

"Pray," Marcie said, on a lighter note, "do not bother yourself on my account. I am perfectly able to find my own space."

"And where might that be?" Cole Coachman demanded, clearly in a hurry to get a move on.

"Why, near the hind boot, alongside your good guard, John Reeve." She lifted her chin defiantly. "You will find that I am most adept at hanging on for dear life should you continue to take the turns as though the hounds of hell are charging after us."

With that, Marcie turned away and commenced to climb aboard the back of the carriage, the sound of Cole Coachman's exasperated sigh ringing in her ears.

She'd successfully—and rather stubbornly—wound a sturdy strap about her gloved wrist when Cole Coachman came tearing round the carriage, his eyes ablaze.

He pulled her hand free of the strap. "Of all the scatterbrained, ninnyhammered ideas!" he groused.

"I beg your pardon?"

"I've no doubt that you do, but I'll not be having you trailing my coach like some rag doll flapping in the breeze. If you refuse to take a seat inside, then I must insist you ride with me on the box."

He did not allow her the chance to argue.

Marcie was forced to stumble along behind the broad-shouldered form of Cole Coachman. He half led, half dragged Marcie to the front of the coach where he immediately hoisted her into the air and atop the bench with no more exertion than if he'd been tossing a bag of seed onto a farmer's cart.

Marcie landed with a thud on the hard wood. "This is hardly necessary," she gasped.

"Not in my viewpoint, it isn't," he muttered, heading round the horses, and checking the sturdiness of their reins as he went. He then climbed up beside her, reached for his long whip, set his fine team to motion.

Marcie was forced back as the spirited horses took off in a flurry of spitting snow.

And so it was that Marcie joined Cole Coachman on the bench, and found herself squinting into the slanting snowfall and braving chilling winds, while Miss Deirdre and Nan no doubt shared yet another box of bonbons within the warm comfort of the coach.

So much for famous beginnings, thought Marcie sourly. She snuggled deep into her pelisse, and soundly cursed every moment following her unfortunate meeting with the moody Cole Coachman. The inn at Burford could not come soon enough!

Four

Cole Coachman—*né* the Marquis of Sherringham—found himself wondering how in the blazes he'd acquired not one, but two extra passengers on this madcap Mail run. Doubtless his contemporaries in Town, should they ever get wind of the antics of this night—which, of course, Cole would see to it they never did—would share many hearty laughs, all at his expense.

Miss Marcie huddled against the cold, and locked her eyes to the distant and snow-obscured horizon. No doubt she was counting the miles until she could be free of both himself and their newly acquired passenger. Perhaps she was even wondering why Cole had acquiesced and allowed Miss Deirdre more than ample space within his overburdened coach.

The answer was, quite simply, that Miss Deirdre Winnifred Waxford was none other than the latest swan to capture the interest of the Prince Regent. It wouldn't do at all for Sherringham to allow such a woman to flounder along a dangerous road. B'gad, but being a gentleman was deuced inconvenient at times!

As for the mischievous young miss he'd acquired from some snowy mews . . . well, she was another matter entirely. Imagine, her thinking she would latch herself near the hind boot alongside Reeve!

What a stubborn chit she could be, thought Cole, chancing a glance at her from the corners of his eyes. She sat ramrod straight on the bench, her gloved hands folded upon her lap, eyes slanted against the snow, her chin held in that defiant position Cole was coming to know all too well. She hadn't uttered a word of discomfort. She'd not made a fuss about the wind slicing through her hair and doubtless chilling her to the bone. Indeed, she now appeared quite fully prepared to endure the violent weather and was making a famous attempt to ignore all the discomforts the bench afforded her, which were many.

Dash it all, thought Cole, but the maddening miss was beginning to grow on him. He rather liked her spiritedness, found her self-sufficient attitude most refreshing. And blazes, but those bewitching green eyes—catching the glow of the running lamps were far too appealing by all accounts.

It was a mystery to him why he'd even bothered to help her as much as he had. The Marquis of Sherringham, though constantly bending to the demanding wills of his many nieces and sisters-in-law, had actually made a name for himself in Town as being a bit of a curmudgeon. Indeed, there were those of the ton who termed him a stuffy bore, for he rarely bothered himself with anyone that caused him the slightest bit of trouble. No doubt the reason for this was that he had more than enough on his plate with his overly demanding family.

But perhaps his behavior more truly derived from the fact that Cole had ever been third choice in his now deceased father's eyes. It was no secret to one and all that Cole had forever lived in the shadow of his elder brothers. He'd been forever second best to those two lively, handsome gentlemen, who set the ton all astir with their quick wit and startling good looks.

It smarted Cole to know that, should his eldest brother, Harry, not have been taken from life by illness, and his second eldest brother, George, not have been struck down and killed by a runaway carriage, he himself would no doubt still be living in their shadows. To ascend to one's title only because one had managed, by sheer luck of the draw, to outlive two seemingly healthy bucks was something Cole hadn't quite learned to deal with. He would have rather taken his title by storm. Instead, he took it cloaked in mourning garb and with a somberness he could not shake.

It was the memory of his brothers—teasing brutes though they might have been, but beloved nonetheless—that made Cole care for both their offspring and their widows as well. And though all the females left to his care seemed bent on bleeding him dry and testing his mettle, Cole strove to please them all.

Of course, all that pleasing left far too little time for himself . . . and now, here he was, taking on yet another unprotected female. Three, he corrected himself quickly, counting his half sister, Nan, as well as the golden-haired Miss Deirdre.

Trouble was, Cole was a mite too interested in the mischievous Miss Marcie. There was something about her . . . something sad, but feisty, too. She'd wished to be free of her boarding school, and so she had fled. Simple as that! Cole admired that. Too, there seemed to be a life-loving air about her. She appeared quite determined to enjoy herself no matter what.

Cole deduced he should keep his mind on his team and the road before him, not on the runaway school girl beside him. So thinking, he set his face into grim lines and concentrated on a tricky bend ahead.

* * *

An hour later, the snowfall lessened to nothing more than huge, lazy flakes of pristine white twirling to the ground. The twisting and hazardous turns of road gave way to a wide berth that stretched endlessly before them. There appeared a full moon in the sky, its phosphorescent beams painting the landscape in a bluish haze.

The beauty of the silent night near took Cole's breath away. Such precious, quiet moments were the reason he took his duties in the Whip Driving Club so seriously. Only on the open road could a man find such solitude. London, with its mad pace and narrow lanes, seemed far, far away.

The young woman beside him, as though reading his thoughts, finally spoke.

"How lovely," she said, motioning to a passing grove of pines hooped and bowed with snow. "It is so peaceful in the country. Nothing like Town, with all its hubbub and coal smoke."

"You do not care for the city?" he asked.

"Oh, I like it well enough," Miss Marcie replied, "but only in small doses. Everyone is always in such a hurry. They seem to have nothing better to do than rush to a party, and pass along tidbits of gossip." She sighed. "I rather prefer wide open spaces. I find a walk in the fresh air more to my liking than a crowded drawing room."

"As do I," agreed Cole.

She tipped her face up to his. "How marvelous for you, then, that you constantly find yourself racing along these enchanting roads. What I would not give to be as free!"

Free? thought Cole. Oh, if she only knew how very tied up he was with matters of his inheritance and with his demanding sisters-in-law, Patricia and Laurinda, and their many daughters!

"I was not always so shackled," she murmured, turning her pretty face back to the road stretching out before them.

"No?"

"Not at all," she admitted. "There was a time when I was as free as a bird, allowed to flutter where I wished . . . but that was before my father—before he died."

"I am sorry," said Cole softly, "that your father has passed away."

She bowed her head momentarily. "He was a very sweet man. He fussed over me, certainly, but he also possessed sense enough to realize I needed to find my own place in this wide world of ours. He was . . . very good at allowing me to discover my own inner strengths."

Cole had guessed as much. Not every female would take kindly to being transported aboard a Mail coach, nor would an ordinary female accept—let alone adapt to—finding herself traveling atop a hard bench and braving a wicked snowstorm.

"I take it you haven't lived all of your life in Town," said Cole.

"Not at all." Melancholy forgotten, she lifted her face, eyes suddenly bright. "I was reared in the West Country. Cornwall, to be exact. Have you ever been to Cornwall?"

He shook his head.

"Pity that. You do not know what you are missing."

"Then do tell," he urged, quite taken by the bright gleam in her green eyes.

Miss Marcie hastened to share her memories. "The sound of the sea crashes endlessly in one's ears. And the gulls! What a song their cries create. There are many cliffs, each

one with a stunning view. All the roads seem to lead to and
from the sea, and there is always a breeze blowing.

"As a child, I used to think that every blowing breeze
carried memories of those who have gone before us. It was
a silly thought, I know, but one that never ceased to amaze
me. I could often imagine hearing the sound of a pirate's
cutlass hissing in the air, or the lonely call of a siren's song
chanting in the winds. I used to ride my pony along the
rocky shores, hunting smuggler's hiding-holes of long ago,
and finding footprints in the sand that I thought surely must
belong to a famous smuggler!"

Cole laughed with her at her lovely daydreams of youth.
"Ah, you are a dreamer, then," he said.

"No," she replied, softly, surely. "I am a believer." She
shivered then, though just barely.

Cole immediately chastised himself. How very remiss of
him not to see to her need for warmth. He was, after all,
fenced in a warm coat and several layers of clothing.

"You are cold," he murmured.

He reached beneath the bench with his right hand and
pulled out the thick carriage rug he'd tucked there at the
beginning of his Mail run.

"Here," he said, shaking the blanket open with one strong
yank, then fluttering it over and atop her knees.

She accepted the rug with good grace, but said, "There
is no need for you to go out of your way on my behalf.
Truly, I am quite comfortable. Indeed, I rather prefer riding
on the bench to being enclosed in the coach."

Cole thought her to be too much on her manners at that
moment. He might have told her as much, but in the next
instant, the young woman sat straight up on the bench and
clapped her hands to her chest, the carriage rug slipping
woefully down to puddle at her feet.

"Oh! Look!" she cried.

Cole feared she'd spied a highwayman lurking in the shadows. He too quickly ground his team to a shattering stop along the road.

"What?" he gasped, ready to reveal his gun should the need arise.

The young woman abruptly shushed him, then said, "There! Hidden in yonder snowbank. Do you see?"

Cole could see nothing more than the broad sweep of snow and endless night. It would not surprise him if a band of thieves lay in wait, "hidden in yonder snowbank."

So thinking, he reached for his gun, giving signal to Reeve to do the same, and all the while glad for the young miss's sharp eye.

"Whatever you do, do not make any sudden moves," he said softly to Miss Marcie.

"Oh, I shan't," she whispered in reply, her gaze fixed on the snowbank just ahead.

"My guard and I have things well in hand," he said.

"I've no doubt you do, but if you would lend me your gauntlet, I am certain I could take care of this matter all on my own." This she said just as Cole aimed his weapon on the snowbank in question.

Gauntlet?

"What the devil are you talking about?" Cole demanded.

Obviously distracted by his questioning, the young miss glanced quickly over at him and, seeing his weapon, gave a cry of dismay.

"Oh, but you couldn't . . . wouldn't!"

She lunged for his gun.

Cole found himself pressed bodily back on the bench as Miss Marcie, in a very unladylike manner, thrust the weapon from his hands. He allowed her her head only because he didn't fashion having the gun triggered and thus sending a round of shot into the rump of one of his horses! Too, he'd come to the conclusion there must not be any thieves or highwaymen lurking in the shadows. And if there were, they no doubt would have sense enough to tuck tail and run rather than meet with the likes of one Marcelon Victoria Darlington.

Cole found himself smothered beneath the lithe form of the very indignant and far too spirited school girl. Unfortunately for Cole, he found her body warm and soft and far too appealing.

John Reeve took that moment to come racing forward, pistol in hand.

"I feared there was trouble brewing," said John Reeve, clearly not at all pleased to have been alerted from his perch and urged to pull his pistol for naught.

Both Cole and Miss Marcie lifted their heads, peering down at the disgruntled guard.

Cole frowned.

"Thank goodness you've come," said Miss Marcie, disentangling herself from Cole. "Perhaps you can talk some sense into your coachman, as he seems to be of the mind to murder a poor, helpless owl!"

That said, she tossed Cole's gun down to John Reeve.

The guard caught it easily.

Marcie smiled at him.

The guard tipped up his hat with the barrel of the gun, smiling back at her.

"Mayhap you'll be needing me glove to scoop up that owl and place him out of harm's way, mistress," said John Reeve, sounding sweeter than Cole had ever heard the man sound.

"Indeed I shall," replied Miss Marcie.

She took the proffered glove, then turned a heated gaze toward Cole.

"You could learn a thing or two from your guard, Cole Coachman," she scolded. "If you had given me your gauntlet when I first asked, we could have totally avoided this . . . this sorry incident. Imagine! Aiming your weapon at an owl!"

Cole, sprawled on the seat, scratched his head in dismay as Miss Marcie turned away, deftly jumped down from the bench, then carefully proceeded toward an injured owl, which was by now clearly visible to Cole. And to think he'd only meant to save her from scoundrels! What an impertinent—not to mention thankless—little chit she could be! Cole sat up, readjusted his greatcoat, then turned his attention to John Reeve.

The man scowled up at him.

"I didn't see any owl," Cole said, feeling a preposterous need to explain himself.

"Obviously," intoned Reeve. He sniffed, clearly put out.

Cole ignored the reaction. "My gun, Reeve, and be quick about it."

John Reeve reluctantly handed up the weapon, then turned and headed for the hind boot, all the while muttering about high-handed swells and their idiotic notions of manning Mail carriages.

Cole quelled the urge to pull rank on both the cranky guard and the mischievous Miss Marcie. He had a sinking feeling it would do him no good.

Just then, the carriage door popped open and Nan stuck her head out into the chill night air.

"Marcie isn't sick again, is she?" she asked.

"Lord, I hope not," groused Cole. He was beginning to feel a bit sick himself, with all these starts and stops, compliments of none other than Miss Marcie.

"Then why have we stopped?" Nan whined.

Why indeed? thought Cole. He had only to glance in Miss

Marcie's direction to have his answer. The female had not only lifted the broken-winged owl from its snowbank perch, but was carrying the creature toward the coach.

"Absolutely not," said Cole, shaking his head. "You'll not be bringing an owl aboard this coach, mistress."

"But he's wounded and hungry," Miss Marcie countered. "Surely you cannot object, nor could you possibly expect me to leave him in some barren tree to fend for himself. He has broken a wing!"

She moved to the carriage door, asking Nan to pass out a sweetmeat. Nan eagerly obliged, all the while clucking over the little bird. She gave Miss Marcie the desired sweetmeat, then leaned out the door to coo some more over the creature.

"Is it not the most adorable little thing you've ever seen, Cole?" asked Nan.

Cole frowned at his flighty half sister. " 'Tis a barn owl, Nan. It feeds on rodents and would as soon nip off your fingertip as look at you."

"Nonsense," Miss Marcie intervened. "He appears harmless enough. And just look how beautiful its plumage is! It appeared pure white against the snow bank, but now I can clearly see it is actually specked with brown. I think it is the most beautiful bird I've ever held."

Cole watched as Miss Marcie tipped her head to peer at the monkey-faced owl. A few curls escaped her bonnet, wisping against her cheek and fluttering in the cold breeze. She ran the fingertips of her free hand across the owl's head, gently ruffling the feathers there. Cole was not surprised to hear the owl emit a soft "snore" of pleasure.

A curious ache stirred in his chest. He found himself wondering what precious pets she might have been forced to leave behind when she'd traveled to that odious school from which he'd whisked her away. She'd mentioned a pony she'd often ridden along the sands of Cornwall, and she'd talked of screeching gulls as though they'd been dear friends. Cole had no doubt but that Miss Marcie must have nurtured a good many broken-winged birds during her girlhood in Cornwall.

Looking at her now, with her head bent, a few soft ringlets framing her radiant face, he saw, suddenly, not a mischievous chit who had taken great delight in scampering away from her rigid boarding school; rather, he beheld a beauteous young woman who had, perhaps, had her own wings broken a time or two.

"Can we not take the owl with us?" asked Miss Marcie, the sound of her pretty voice cutting into Cole's wandering thoughts.

"Oh, yes, please!" chimed in Nan.

Cole scowled. He was an hour behind schedule. This mail run was becoming ridiculously muddled with all sorts of complications. Take an owl aboard the coach? It was a preposterous notion! Thoroughly ridiculous.

Cole glared down at Miss Marcie, prepared to gainsay her. One look into the jewel-like facets of her eyes, though, weakened his resolve.

"Devil take it," he groused. "Climb back aboard the coach, mistress, and bring that blasted owl with you if you must."

Nan let out a cry of glee, handing Marcie an entire box of unopened sweetmeats.

Miss Marcie, hiding a pleased smile, took the sweetmeats, then climbed back onto the bench, the monkey-faced owl looking complacent, spoilt, and far too content.

"Thank you, Cole Coachman," murmured Miss Marcie.

"Yes . . . well . . . ahem," muttered Cole. "You are quite welcome," he said, adding, "I think."

And then they were off, heading into the eerily lit night: a swell coachman, a mail guard, a seamstress's daughter, a lover of the Prince Regent, a broken-winged owl . . . and one very precocious, runaway schoolgirl.

Who would have thought Cole Coachman, *né* the Marquis of Sherringham, had intended only to race the Valentine's Day mails to the Cotswolds?

Five

"I think I shall name him Prinny," announced Marcie, several miles later.

"Eh? What's that you say?" asked Cole Coachman.

Caught up in racing the coach along tricky roads, the handsome man had obviously quite forgotten not only Marcie's presence, but the owl's as well. No matter. Marcie, intrigued by the bird perched so complacently on her arm, had actually forgotten her earlier pique at being forced to sit atop the bench while Miss Deirdre and Nan snuggled beneath warm carriage rugs inside the coach. Too, she found the silence between herself and the coachman to be a most comfortable thing. The man wasted no energy on making small talk. This pleased Marcie. She was not one to waste words either, nor mince them, for that matter.

"My new friend," she explained to Cole Coachman. "I've decided he looks very much like a 'Prinny' to me."

"How so?"

"Well, for one, he is very regal, don't you agree? And he *is* plump."

Cole Coachman gave her and the bird a quick glance. "I s'pose the fact you have given him a name indicates you intend to claim him as your own?"

"Why ever would you suppose that? Really, sir, I would not presume to claim ownership on anything or anyone. To do so would be, in my opinion, quite arrogant. I only meant that I shall think of this bird as Prinny. As for my keeping him, that is solely Prinny's choice. He can stay, or he can go."

"And if he does not choose to stay?"

"Then I shall bid him a fond farewell," Marcie replied easily. "After all, life is naught but a series of meetings and partings. Don't you agree?"

"You speak as though you've experienced one too many partings."

"I have had two too many partings," she said softly, honestly. "My mother and my father."

"Forgive me." Cole felt beastly. "I did not mean to bring about sad memories."

"Pray, do not apologize," Marcie said quickly, smiling up into his handsome face. "The memory of my parents is sweet, not sad. And I like to remember them. Indeed, I hope never to forget them. Not that I could. Though our time together was far too short, it was wonderful and unforgettable. If I learned nothing else from them, I learned that life is indeed precious and far too brief. That is why I've decided to name this feathered creature."

Cole shook his head. "I'm afraid you have quite befuddled me now."

"I doubt that." Marcie grinned. "I do not think you are so easily befuddled, Cole Coachman."

"Please, call me Cole. Cole Coachman sounds far too stuffy."

"And an experienced coachman such as yourself would hate to be thought of as stuffy?"

"Something like that," he replied, his voice curiously tight.

"Very well, then . . . Cole. The reason I've named this bird is because I enjoy giving names to persons, animals or things that bring me joy. For instance, I have a name for every fossil I carry in my portmanteau."

"Surely you are jesting."

"No, I am not," Marcie said, her smile broadening at his gentle tone. "I am quite serious. I found one fossil in a smuggler's cave. I call that fossil 'Ship's End,' because it is very large, with many distinguishing marks, and would make a tidy landmark for someone looking for such a thing. I like to think that a ship's captain would traverse the seas looking for such a fossil. It is a Valentine's Day gift for my cousin, Mirabella, as I do believe she has long been travelling the world in search of a sturdy landing place. I've another fossil for my other cousin, Meredith, who is ever so lovely. This fossil is smaller than the others but imprinted with many figures. You see, Merry—or rather, Meredith—has the ability to see into another person's soul. I thought this puzzle of a fossil would be the perfect gift for her. As for our mutual friend, Nan, I haven't a fossil for her, but I do delight in calling her Mistress Busybody."

"I well know why!" Cole laughed. "And John Reeve?" he asked, sobering somewhat. "Have you a special name for him?"

Marcie smothered a giggle. "I shouldn't admit it," she said.

"Do tell."

"I think of him as 'Sir General.' A mix of military and nobility."

"Oh, he is that, to be sure." Cole grinned. Then, of a sudden, and rather haltingly, he asked, "And me, Miss Marcie?"

"Please, if I am to address you as Cole, then you must call me Marcie," she said.

"Consider it done. And what of me, Marcie? Have you

thought of a name that suits me?" He gazed at her, his gray eyes clear and unutterably mesmerizing.

Marcie blushed. Blast, but the man had a way causing her to feel both excitement and confusion, not to mention an odd sort of vulnerability.

"To be quite frank?" she asked.

"To be very frank," he said.

Marcie took a deep breath, then plunged ahead. "I think of you as 'My Lord Monarch.' "

Cole Coachman threw back his head and laughed.

"You do appear to be quite decisive and set in your ways," she answered honestly. "You don't like surprises, do you?"

His laughter eased. "No. I do not."

"Everything in its place, and a place for everything, am I correct?"

"Precisely correct."

Marcie nodded. "I thought as much," she said, then grimaced. "I can only guess what name you've given *me,* then. I have certainly made a mess of your time schedule."

"Indeed you have."

"And have you, My Lord Monarch, attached a name to me? Surely, you've one swimming in that head of yours."

"Oh, I do at that. Mistress Mischief. For obvious reasons."

Marcie bowed her head, quickly hiding the shimmer of tears that suddenly sprang to her eyes and tickled her eyelids. Only one other person had ever called her Mistress Mischief.

"I have offended you," he said, obviously misunderstanding her reaction.

Marcie blinked away the wetness from her eyes. She looked up at him. "Quite the opposite. You see, my father used to call me Mistress Mischief."

"It seems I am forever stirring up memories for you."

"Yes," she whispered. "It does seem that way, doesn't it?" And as she spoke, she felt a tiny tremor of feeling inside her breast, a feeling she could not quite express. Happiness at the memory of her father? Yes, it was that . . . and yet it was so much more complicated, and had more to do with the man seated beside her.

Cole Coachman smiled at her, reaching over with one gloved hand to pull up the carriage rug that was threatening to puddle down around her toes once again.

"Wouldn't want you to catch your death," he murmured.

His gloved hand brushed against her own, and Marcie felt a shiver tingle up her spine. Of a sudden, she could not help but notice how very near he was. She could smell the crisp, clean scent of him, and the delicious smell of cedar emanating from his greatcoat and red scarf. The world sped past as the coach whisked over the road, and to Marcie it seemed as if there was only just herself, Cole Coachman, and Prinny alive in the universe. What a very cosy place it was.

The blare of a horn brought Marcie abruptly out of her reverie.

"Heavens!" cried Marcie, startled. "What is that?"

Cole Coachman chuckled. " 'Tis only our guard alerting those at the upcoming post of our arrival."

"What post?" asked Marcie.

Even as she said the words, they rounded a bend, and up ahead, in the distance, could be seen a glare of lights through ice-laden tree branches.

"What a sight!" she exclaimed as Cole Coachman expertly slowed his team through a narrow gateway, then into a well-lit coachyard. The glare of torches stung her eyes, and the shouts of "Hallo!" and "Welcome!" from ostlers and a burly aproned man, who could only be master of the inn, became music to her ears.

"We will not stay long," Cole Coachman said. He brought the horses to a halt, put away his silver-mounted whip, then dropped down off the bench. "Reeve and I have the transfer of packages and letters to make. There'll also be a change of horses. Shouldn't take us longer than fifteen minutes. Perhaps less." He nodded toward the door of the small and very quaint inn. "You will find hot, sweet tea, and perhaps a sweetcake or two inside. But try not to tarry too long."

"Oh, I shan't," Marcie assured him. She was down off the bench even before he could step around and offer his assistance. Prinny rustled his feathers but made no motion to remove himself from his perch on her shoulder.

John Reeve was already making fast work of tossing down the mail bags intended for this stop. Cole Coachman, surrounded now by three ostlers, gave the order for a fresh team of horses.

Marcie, hoping to make herself useful, decided she should alert Nan and Miss Deirdre of their stop. She found the two women sound asleep in the coach.

"Psst," Marcie said, peeking her head inside the carriage door.

Nan popped one bleary eye open.

"We've time enough to stretch our legs, if you're of a mind to do so," whispered Marcie.

Nan wrinkled her pert nose, shaking her head. "La, Marcie, I was dreaming of a handsome prince, I was." Squashed between a mountain of boxes and packages, and very happily so, she snuggled deeper into the squabs. "There is no way I will leave my dreams to venture out into the cold!"

"Not even for some hot, sweet tea?" Marcie coaxed.

"Not even," muttered Nan, falling fast asleep again.

Marcie glanced over at Miss Deirdre. That one was also

fast asleep, stretched out luxuriously on the opposite seat, covered from nose to toes in a thick rug.

Marcie shrugged and quietly closed the carriage door.

"I guess it is just the two of us, Prinny," she said to the owl. With that, she headed for the door of the inn.

The building was squat and rather small. A bit rustic, too, but the lights burning inside and the sparkling ice hanging in perfect cones from its pitched roof made it appear quite inviting. Marcie no sooner reached for the latch of the door than the portal was thrust open and a behemoth of a woman stood in its frame to greet her.

"We've been waiting for your coach," said the woman in a loud, firm voice. "Expected you several hours ago. No trouble along the road, was there? No thieves to hinder your progress? No accidents?"

"Only one," said Marcie, feeling guilty as she remembered once again how Miss Deirdre's driver had run his carriage into a snowbank. "But all is well," she hastened to add. Cole Coachman had already delivered the tale of Miss Deirdre's driver to the ostlers, even while he'd commenced to oversee the change of horses. Help would soon be sent to Miss Deirdre's driver.

"Well, then, do come in, Missy. Why, your nose is as red as a cherry, and your cheeks pink. Do not tell me the handsome Cole Coachman forced you to sit atop his bench with him! Lordy, but Cole must think everyone likes to freeze alongside him."

Marcie smiled. "I did so on my accord, truly."

"Ah, a brave miss, are you? Good! Come, warm your bones by the fire. I got some sweetcakes warming on the stove, just the way Cole likes them to be when he passes through."

Marcie found herself being relieved of her bonnet and pelisse, gloves and tippet—but not before placing Prinny on the top rung of the hat rack near the door. The woman did not seem to think a girl with her owl was an oddity. With much fuss, the woman led Marcie toward the warm fireplace and seated her on a bench there.

Prinny, from his perch, watched with wide-eyed interest as Marcie was quickly served an entire plate of sweetcakes, as well as a mug of steaming tea. Marcie enjoyed the feast, all the while listening to the woman's chatter.

Her name was Meg, Marcie learned. She'd been born and raised at the inn, which had been owned by her father and his father before him. Her husband ran the inn now, and Meg took great delight in serving nourishing meals and keeping the few rooms upstairs neat and tidy.

"Ain't never met a coachman better than Cole," said Meg as she sat down on a stool across from Marcie. She took up a bit of knitting, needles clacking furiously, as she continued speaking. "He be a gentleman, though I do declare he is a bit too serious for his own good. Something about him makes me think he is hiding secrets in his heart."

"Oh?" said Marcie, instantly curious. "Why do you say that?"

"Well, for one, he only comes by once a year, sometimes twice a year, unlike most other coachmen who come through here often. He ain't like other coachmen, though. He don't put on airs—though he could—and we would still race to do his bidding. There be something special about him, and lonely, too. It's as though he took to the roads to find something . . . or someone." Meg shook her head, studying her knitting. "Don't misunderstand me. I've a warm spot in this old heart of mine for Cole Coachman. Most women do—Lordy, *all* women do! But still, he does seem lonely to me. Too lonely for a man as handsome and sweet as he is."

Marcie found herself nodding in agreement, and once again a queer warm feeling tingled up her spine. She finished most of the tea, and ate too many sweetcakes. Then Meg insisted that Marcie follow her. Marcie was led to a warm room at the back of the inn, one with a washstand and a pitcher of tepid water.

"No doubt you'll be wanting to freshen up a bit before Cole decides to put you back on that hard bench of his," said Meg, closing the door and leaving Marcie alone.

Marcie wasted no time in taking up the woman's offer. She washed her face and hands, tidied her hair, then finished her ablutions, feeling a world better as she retraced her steps back to the common room.

Cole and John Reeve were standing near the fire, warming their bodies and drinking a tankard of Meg's special hot-buttered rum.

"Feeling better?" asked Cole.

Marcie nodded.

"Good. We've made the transfer and must be setting off again," he said. He finished off the tankard, then reached for his gloves.

Meg fussed and mussed over him, even going so far as to wrap up several sweetcakes into a square of snowy linen for him. Into the top button of his greatcoat, she placed an early-flowering primrose.

"My way of saying happy Saint Valentine's Day to you."

Cole surprised—and pleased—the older woman by planting a quick kiss on her plump cheek. "And to you," he said. He reached inside his pocket and pulled forth a prettily wrapped package.

Meg cooed with delight, tearing open the package to find two new knitting needles. She began to cry.

Cole Coachman lifted one hand and gently dashed away

a tear with his thumb. "I hadn't meant to make you cry, Meg," he said.

Meg waved one hand at him, crying all the more. "Scat, then, before you see me cry a bucketful of tears! Though I've nourished a legion of coachmen, not a one has thought to bring me such a gift. God bless you, Cole Coachman."

"And God bless you, Meg, for you've warmed my heart with your light banter and generous ways. Too, I love your sweetcakes."

Meg blushed, looking like a schoolgirl, though she was a woman grown and wizened by life. "Go on," she said. "Get. And be sure to stop here on your way back to London. I promise to have a feast prepared for you on your way back through."

"It is a date I will race to make, Meg." Cole then made a motion towards the door. John Reeve was the first to move, nodding his thanks to both the innkeeper and to Meg.

Marcie, however, found herself quite rooted to her spot. She was gazing at Cole. He was framed by firelight, his muscled form clearly outlined, and his face made even more handsome by the genuine friendship he felt for the woman named Meg.

The man was indeed a puzzle, thought Marcie. He could be cold and gruff as well as warm and wonderful. He could bark about being behind schedule, but could just as easily take time to retrieve a broken-winged bird from the roadside and gift a gabby innkeeper's wife with a new set of knitting needles.

Too, he'd helped a runaway schoolgirl escape from the snowy mews of a London boarding school. Never would Marcie forget that.

"Are you ready?" Cole was asking her.

Marcie yanked her thoughts back to the present. "More than ready, My Lord Monarch," she said, a smile on her lips.

Cole Coachman gifted her with a grin. Indeed, he even took it upon himself to guide Prinny from his hat-rack perch. Prinny went easily enough but ruffled his feathers as Marcie stepped beside Cole.

"You had best take him. He seems to be particular about where he deigns to perch."

Marcie took the bird, which hopped atop her muff, and stayed there until Cole helped her up and onto the hard bench, at which time Prinny jumped down to sit in the space between her body and Cole's.

Waving to Meg and the innkeep, Marcie found herself thrust back on the seat as Cole directed his horses out of the yard and back onto the road.

John Reeve blew his horn once again.

And once again, the silence and beauty of the eerily lit night took them into its depths.

Marcie found herself nodding off to sleep, huddled as she was beneath the toasty carriage rug. She felt warm and safe with Prinny perched at her side and "whoo-whooing" now and then. The sound of the carriage wheels churning over the snow-covered roads lulled her into a peaceful state, and the sound of Cole Coachman's even breathing helped propel her into a soft cocoon of dreamy wonder.

And what dreams she had!

She dreamed of a castle carved out of dark stone. Caught in the depths of its chilling darkness, she could suddenly hear the thunder of pounding horses' hooves, could feel the very earth tremble. A bold knight in a blazing chariot materialized, racing toward her. Yet there came a villain as well. Marcie heard the snort of the villain's black beast, could feel the man's menace from a universe away. She saw herself reaching for the shining white knight. Just another few paces and she would be beside him. One more step, and then all would be well . . . .

Marcie came awake with a start, feeling horridly compelled to scream. Her eyes opened to the glare of torchlight. The coach wasn't moving, and she felt Cole's rigid body next to hers.

"What . . . ?" she began.

"Hush," Cole whispered forcefully.

What had seemed a dream, wasn't totally a dream. The coach had indeed stopped. She spied the gun in Cole's hands. Looking up, she saw the rider upon which that gun was aimed.

"Stand and deliver!" called the dark and menacing figure positioned before them on the road.

It was a highwayman barring their way! And he held a primed pistol pointing straight at Marcie's heart.

"Do not move," muttered Cole.

Marcie nodded, forcing herself not to breathe.

Even Prinny came awake then, widening his large eyes and peering at the lone rider.

"I be holding me barker," said the masked man. "Now hand over yer valuables. Yer jewels, mate, or I blow a hole clean through yer lady friend afore you can move!"

Marcie, now fully awake, found herself miffed that the lowly man would dare to threaten Cole. Too, the fact that the robber's hand shook a bit as he tossed out his horrid threat made her think the man was not the terrible beastie he hoped they would believe him to be.

He wore a threadbare coat, several sizes too big, and a dirty muffler which he'd wound about the lower half of his face. His boots were scuffed and dirty and worn through at the toes, at which place he'd tied some strips of old cloth. His fingers stuck through the knitting of his gloves, and his slouch hat was much the worse for wear.

A very unlikely highwayman, thought Marcie. Having been reared in Cornwall, she'd viewed—from afar, of course—more than a few highway thieves. The man did not at all seem cut out for a life of thievery and mayhem—or murder, for that matter. Too, didn't highwaymen steal enough coin to dress themselves in a warm fashion?

"Now, see here," said Cole in a low and lethal voice. "I could shoot out your left eye before you even have a chance to pull the trigger. If I were you, sir, I would think twice about trying to shoot the lady."

"Well, you ain't me," snapped the man, his scratchy voice wavering. "And I be holding up this coach. Now do as I say!"

"Like hell I will," said Cole Coachman.

Marcie panicked. She had to do something. Anything!

But Prinny took that moment to hop up onto her lap. "Oh, Prinny, no!" she cried, hoping the owl's movement didn't cause the highwayman to shoot. She reached to capture the owl.

Too late!

The owl, frightened by her quick movement, took that moment to test its broken wing. It fluttered up and off her lap, landing haphazardly on the slouch hat of the highwayman with much flapping of its wings.

"Awk!" squealed the highwayman. "Have ye sent the devil to plague me? Call him off! Call him off, I say!"

The man dropped his gun, which landed innocently enough on the ground. John Reeve, having jumped down from the hind boot when the coach stopped, moved to scoop up the weapon. He cocked it open.

"It was never loaded!" he cried, staring up in dismay at Cole Coachman, who shook his head and muttered a curse.

Marcie, however, found her thoughts solely on Prinny.

"Oh, you silly bird," she chided, climbing down off the bench, then reaching up to retrieve the owl from the highwayman's head.

"La! He done scratched me face, he did!" cried the highwayman.

Marcie managed to calm the man's weather-worn horse even while coaxing Prinny to perch on her shoulder.

"If that is all he did, then you should consider yourself fortunate," scolded Marcie. "Imagine, holding up a Royal Mail coach, and threatening to shoot me! Your mother would doubtless turn over in her grave!"

"Oh, pray, miss, do not say such a thing! I loved me mum. She was the bright spot of me sorry youth. I was just hungry. Me horse is hungry, too."

"Well, why didn't you say so?" said Marcie, her tone softening. "We've some sweetcakes on board. And sweetmeats, too. We'll share them, certainly."

"We will?" demanded Cole, glaring down at Marcie.

"Of course we shall," said Marcie, turning round and looking up at Cole. In a whisper, she said, "Can you not see that the man is desperate for food? I dareswear I might be forced to rob a coach should I be caught up in such dire straits!"

Cole released a disgruntled sigh. "No doubt you would, you little mischievous soul," he said.

Marcie ignored his well-intentioned dig. She turned back to the highwayman.

"You haven't another weapon on your person, have you?"

The man bowed his head, his growling stomach obviously getting the best of him. "Only a knife in me boot."

"Hand it over," ordered Marcie. "That is, if you wish to join us. We'll take you to our next stop and see that you have a decent meal, and that your horse has a warm stall."

"You would do that for me?" said the man, amazed.

"Of course," said Marcie. She looked up at Cole. "Won't we, My Lord Monarch?"

"Oh, for the love of—yes, yes, of course," he grumbled. "I've taken up a runaway schoolgirl, an owl, why should I cease my philanthropic acts now?" All of this was highly irregular, but then again so was the fact that Cole had taken the reins of a Royal Mail coach and not a mere stage coach as some swell dragsmen did.

"My exact thoughts," said Marcie, smiling.

"Reeve," Cole ordered, "see the man—" he paused a moment. He turned a stern stare toward the highwayman. "What is your name, man? And don't be giving me any aliases you've doubtless assumed."

The highwayman lifted his grubby face to stare at Cole. "Me true name be John, but me mum always called me Jack."

It seemed an honest enough answer. Cole nodded. To Reeve, he said, "See that Jack has a place to sit."

Reeve shuddered in haughty distaste. "Surely you do not expect me to house him on the hind boot," grumbled he. It was a preposterous notion for any guard worth his salt to allow a stranger to perch in the lofty hind boot, for it was upon that very boot where the guard rode and made a living of protecting the mail bags.

Cole Coachman frowned. "Very well. The thief can sit atop the carriage behind me, but—" Cole glared at the highwayman. "But should he make a motion to unseat me, I'll spare him no mercy."

The highwayman appeared affronted at such a scenario.

"Hitch up his horse, Reeve," bellowed Cole Coachman, "and do not, I pray, take your eyes off the thief."

Reeve moved to do the coachman's bidding.

"Wait!" said Marcie. "Your sweetcakes, Cole. We should offer some to the man now."

Cole frowned, obviously not wanting to have anything to do with a lowly thief and, perhaps, not wishing to part with any of Meg's famous sweetcakes, but the generous spirit of one lovely runaway schoolgirl seemed to be upon him, for he reluctantly reached into his greatcoat and pulled forth the snowy linen Meg had given him.

The highwayman accepted the food with a nod of his dirty head, then, following Reeve's abrupt command, scrambled onto the tiny perch above Marcie and Cole.

Marcie climbed back on the box.

Cole wagged his head at her. "For as long as I live," he muttered, "I shall never forget this night, Mistress Mischief."

Marcie, ever an angel of mercy to injured birds and unfortunate souls, smiled at Cole. The man was truly not as cold and gruff as he liked to pretend. A joyous lightness fluttered inside her as Cole Coachman took the time to help cover her with the carriage rug once again. *Neither shall I forget this night,* she thought to herself. *Neither shall I . . .*

Six

Cole spent the next several miles pondering the amazing fact that although he was woefully behind schedule, had managed to take on a circus-like mix of riders, and was even now sharing his bench with an owl named Prinny, he wasn't in the least bit fuming, fussing, nor even flabbergasted.

Indeed, he felt, well, rather pleased with the events of the night, if one could actually believe that. Which one couldn't, because normally Cole would have been spitting fire to realize his exacting schedule had been so skewered. And the last time one of his coaches had been set upon by a highwayman, Cole had knocked the man senseless and then transported the scoundrel to the nearest magistrate! It was quite a feat that Cole had held both his temper and his tongue to some degree during this entire topsy-turvy night.

Normally, Cole wouldn't be so accepting of inconveniences. His life at Sherringham House in London was one of detailed exactness, and though certainly coupled with unending interruptions by his many nieces and widowed sisters-in-law, he'd always managed to deal with his many duties by being as dour and as stuffy and stiff-hearted as he could possibly be. To be lax in any way would have threatened to bring the entire household crumbling down round his head.

Though he'd allowed his sisters-in-law to constantly bleed

his coffers, and his nieces to take up far too much of his time with their spoiled demands, he'd never allowed them to pierce the prickly crust surrounding his heart. He'd always kept his distance, and his dignity.

Yet in spite of those facts, he was now charging along a darkened roadway, transporting not only his illegitimate half sister, but the Prince Regent's latest love interest, a starving and very inept highwayman, a guard who viewed himself to be above the masses of humanity, and a runaway schoolgirl and her owl named Prinny. And he was actually enjoying himself!

It was not to be believed. Not at all what Cole had planned.

Cole had taken on this ride because he wished to be alone, and because he'd wished to whisk himself out of Town before his sisters-in-law and his many nieces began to pack numerous bags for their Valentine's Day excursion to the Cotswolds and to the home of one eccentric Penelope Barrington, who lived just outside of Stow-on-the-Wold. He knew only too well that once he delivered the last of his parcels at the inn of Burford he would be expected to travel onward to Penelope Barrington's sprawling Cotswold manor house and thus be directly thrust into the company of a Cit heiress, whom he'd never met but whom his sisters-in-law had decided would be the perfect match for him.

Perfect? Cole doubted that. He was not in the least interested in choosing a wife. He'd seen firsthand how petulant and demanding women could be, thanks to his sisters-in-law. Neither Laurinda nor Patricia enjoyed anything that was the least bit challenging. They much preferred amusing themselves with fashion plates and Town gossip rather than a brisk ride in the park or an intricate round of chess playing.

Cole had intended to avoid Laurinda and Patricia's match-making by using his duties in the Whip Driving Club as an excuse not to join them on their trek to Stow, and also as a way of avoiding their plot to pair him with some Cit heiress, who would no doubt prove to be just as spoilt and selfish as the many heiresses he'd encountered thus far.

Yet here he was, heading for Burford, which was but a short distance from Stow and Penelope's house, with a coach filled with queer folk he barely knew. So much for finding time alone and avoiding having to travel to Stow. Adding to all of this was the fact that Cole was hours behind his appointed schedule.

The only nugget of pleasure for him was the fact that Miss Marcie's smile did odd things to his heart. Cole glanced over at the girl he'd termed "Mistress Mischief." She was mischievous, certainly. But she was also a great deal more, he was beginning to learn.

The fact that she was now sound asleep, snuggled back on the bench, afforded Cole the leisure of admiring the way her fiery curls framed her lovely face, the way her slumbering mouth formed a perfect Cupid's bow, and the way the dusky length of her long, luscious lashes curved upward.

Hers was certainly a face for a locket, he thought. She was far too pretty to be out and about, alone in the world. Someone should be watching over the girl. Someone should safeguard her, he thought.

Cole turned his attention back to the road, minding the bends and ruts. Though he'd been surprised—and concerned—about the way in which his Mistress Mischief had chosen to deal with the highwayman, he'd soon found himself admiring her spunk.

Cole chuckled to himself, shaking his head at the memory of Marcie jumping down off the bench to confront the highwayman. Such a glorious sight! She was brave, he'd give her that. Maybe too brave.

Cole looked over at her once again. The rug had slipped down past her knees again, he realized. Would she never be able to keep it tight about her?

Cole reached over to pull the thing back up and around her. "My little Mistress Mischief," he whispered softly as he tucked the rug around her. "Why ever did no one teach you to beware the chilled and coldhearted souls of this world?"

Surely the girl's spirit would be broken by the scoundrels scouring the earth. Surely her sweet heart would one day be nicked by those people whose souls had been turned to so much brittle, cold stone by the wickedness of the world. People like Jack the highwayman.

Like himself.

Marcie came awake just as Cole Coachman tucked the carriage rug about her. "Hullo," she said sleepily. "I must have drifted off again."

The man quickly pulled his hand away, suddenly concentrating on the reins and muttering something she couldn't make out.

Marcie frowned.

No doubt Cole Coachman was angry with her. She'd been very forward in suggesting that Cole allow the highwayman to board his coach. But even so, Marcie hadn't been able to turn a cold shoulder on the poor little man who'd sought to warm his empty belly by robbing a coach.

"You are not angry with me, are you?" Marcie asked.

He gave her a queer look. "Why ever would you ask that?" he demanded sharply.

Heavens! but the man could be so deuced moody, she thought.

Marcie straightened on the bench. "I guess it must be the way you are gripping the reins," she said, her voice just as sharp. "And your mouth is ever so tight—as though you'd been thinking about how I've made this run such a mess."

"Are you always so forward with everyone you meet?" he demanded.

"Yes," Marcie said. "I am. Now answer my question, if you please."

"And what question was that?"

Marcie gnashed teeth. "Are you angry with me, or not?"

"Would it matter if I were?" he asked, still not looking her in the eye.

"Perhaps," said Marcie. *Definitely,* she thought.

He blew out a long sigh, guiding the coach over a frozen bridge and onto a narrowed lane.

"No, I am not angry," he finally answered. "Though I should warn you to take more care when dealing with ruffians. That highwayman," he muttered, motioning with a nod of his head to the sleeping man behind them, "could have murdered you. I am of the opinion you run pell-mell into every encounter. That is not a very wise thing to do."

"I have never been one to sit back and allow others to chart my course."

"Obviously. But you are naught but a schoolgirl, mistress. And a runaway one at that. Someone must take you to task lest you leap out of the frying pan into the fire."

Marcie felt herself stiffen with anger. "And I suppose you'll next announce that you deem yourself to be that person."

"Little though I like it, yes. The world can be a dangerous place for a schoolgirl on her own."

"I might have been a schoolgirl in London, but we are not in London now. I've left that life behind me, sir. I have no need for a champion, nor even a chaperone, and I take offense that you believe otherwise. I am not as addle-brained as you paint me!"

As she spoke, they turned into the courtyard of a very busy inn. There was much commotion to greet them, with other carriages, carts, barrows, and hackney coaches coming and going, ostlers and porters rushing here and there, and a swarm of sleepy-eyed folk hustling from one conveyance to the next.

Cole Coachman was forced to keep his eye on the bustle surrounding them, as well as on the narrowed lane where he was being flagged to direct the coach. He hadn't a chance to reply to Marcie's heated words, nor did he have the chance to stop her before she scooped up her owl and jumped down off the bench once they'd come to a stop.

Marcie was too angry to look back over her shoulder. So the man thought her to be a flighty schoolgirl, did he? Oooh, but he had made her very angry by saying she was too quick to rush into any situation! What did he know of her childhood, of her life? What did he know what it was like to lose one's parents too soon and be compelled to travel to a strange city to find, not a shimmering future, but instead a horrid schoolmistress and a decrepit schoolhouse filled with odious girls, who constantly teased and belittled her?

Marcie's half-boots clacked atop the ice-encrusted boardwalk as she hastened toward the inn door. She had every intention of staying on at the inn until she could find another coach to transport her to Burford. To hell with the Cole Coachmans of the world, she heatedly thought.

"Thirty minutes!" Cole Coachman called after her; though even this was an outrageous amount of time for a Royal Mail coach to linger at an inn. "This coach leaves for Burford in exactly one half hour. If you are not on board, then we shall depart without you."

Marcie lifted her chin, not looking back.

Let him leave, she thought. She didn't care. The man was far too arrogant and assuming! She would fare far better by ignoring his demands.

And so ignore them she did!

Cole watched in dismay as Marcie marched toward the inn door, head held high. She hadn't even so much as nodded at him. She'd just simply strutted away, with that damnable owl perched on her shoulder.

What an insolent chit she could be.

Not to mention rude.

And obstinate!

And lovely, he thought, watching as she wound her way through the patrons toward the door. The many traveling folk, both young and old, male and female, made way for her, either smiling or tipping their hats. No doubt it was Marcie's ingenuous smile that captured their interests.

And it was that same smile, so sweet and pure, that had captured Cole's heart as well.

"I'll be damned," Cole muttered to himself, quite perplexed, "but she's managed to get under my skin."

"What's that you say?" asked John Reeve, coming to stand beside Cole.

Cole shook the cobwebs from his brain. "Nothing," he said.

"Oh, it be something," said Reeve, a bit too smugly. "And I be thinking it have everything to do with the comely Miss Marcie."

Cole frowned. "The mail, Reeve. Unload, and be quick about it!"

"And what would you like me to do with Jack? Unload him as well?"

Cole lifted one dark brow, watching as the aforementioned man finally awakened, jumped down off the carriage, moved to unhitch his excuse of a horse, and then headed for the stables of the inn.

"I don't think that will be necessary," said Cole. "It seems that our highwayman has made his own decisions. I shall alert the fine keep of this inn as to Jack's straits and will see to it Jack and his horse have enough gold to see them through the remaining winter."

Reeve sniffed, his disapproval of Cole's charity quite obvious. "I have to wonder, my lord—"

"Cole Coachman, you mean," Cole said, glancing about to make certain no one had overheard the slip of Reeve's tongue.

No one had.

"Ahem . . . yes." Reeve sighed, clearly not pleased with the charade. "As I was saying, *Cole Coachman,* I have to wonder at the change come over you."

"Change? I wasn't aware of any change, Reeve. I am the same man I was when we departed Town."

"Oh, to be sure your patience is as thin as ever my lor— Cole Coachman." Here Reeve sniffed again, looking rather put out by Cole's apt demonstration of having little patience. "But your heart has become a might too tender of late."

"And what the devil does that mean?" Cole found himself fast losing what little patience he had left to him.

Said Reeve, in a smug tone of voice, no less, "I never thought I'd live to see the day you took pity upon a highwayman. Why, you're even fussing about the man's miserable horse. Ain't nothing like the Cole Coachman I know."

"How so?" demanded Cole, not at all pleased with Reeve's assessment, but at the same time not about to end the uncomfortable confrontation.

"Testy, aren't we, eh?"

"Not as testy as I'll be if you don't soon come to the point, man!"

Reeve wrinkled his nose. "As I said, your temper is as quick as ever—"

"Never mind that. It is what you said about my heart that has me all ears at the moment, Reeve. Get on with it."

"Very well, then. Your heart, Cole Coachman, seems to have become so much mash during this ride. I do believe Miss Marcie is the cause. You have a fancy for her, haven't you?"

Cole blanched. "Certainly not! The mischievous chit is but a runaway schoolgirl, still wet behind the ears. Why, she's trouble in triplicate. A veritable nuisance!"

"And a very pretty one at that, hmmm?" added Reeve, smiling knowingly.

"She's all of seventeen, if she's a day."

Reeve shrugged. "She's old enough to be on the marriage mart."

"You've overstepped your bounds, Reeve. I'll suffer no more talk about Miss Marcie being anything more to me than just another passenger. I'll transport her to the inn at Burford, and there I shall leave her, mark my words. Is that clear?"

"Clear as bells," said Reeve, tipping up his hat and then turning about to head for the hind boot and the bags of mail there. "Clear as bells ringing amidst a raging thunder storm, that is."

Cole suppressed the very ungentlemanly urge to race after the guard and throttle him soundly. The fact that the carriage door popped open and both Nan and Miss Deirdre were departing the coach, managed to keep Cole's mind centered on the tasks at hand.

He moved toward the door.

Nan had already dropped down to the ground while Miss Deirdre, her long hair all atumble, stood poised in the doorway. She bestowed upon Cole a melting smile.

"What a quaint little inn!" she exclaimed. "You really should have alerted us to our stop," she said. "Perhaps then I would have had time to fix my hair. As it is, I fear I am quite the worse for wear." She made a motion of running long, gloved fingers through her mass of golden curls.

"You look radiant," acknowledged Cole, which she did.

Miss Deirdre's smile widened. Her eyes took on a darker shade as she studied him.

What a supreme flirt she was, thought Cole, knowing only too well how the experienced swans of London Town glided through that sea of excess there. Even so, he took it upon himself to let down the steps and helped to guide Miss Deirdre down to the snow-packed ground.

She leaned a bit too heavily on his arm, all the while fluttering her lashes up at him.

"I dareswear I am quite famished! Please do not say we are stopping at this inn only for the time it takes you and your reliable guard to make the required transport of packages and such, and to change horses. I was so hoping we might all find a moment to partake of a nourishing morsel, something to break the fast, before we must be on our hectic way again."

Cole gently reminded the lovely lady that he was manning a Royal Mail coach, not a luxury carriage.

"Still," said Miss Deirdre, "a few more minutes spent at this quaint inn could not be too much to ask, could it?"

Cole was of the mind to tell the lady her request was indeed too much to ask, when John Reeve, a mail bag slung over his shoulder, sauntered past.

The man tipped his cap. "I be depositing the mail right and quick, Cole Coachman, just as you requested," he said. "I know you're itching to reach Burford, sir. Just like Miss Marcie is. And we wouldn't want to keep Miss Marcie waiting, now would we?" He gave a wink in Cole's direction, then sauntered off.

Cole scowled. Miss Deirdre, however, took John Reeve's show of initiative to mean something altogether different.

"What an industrious servant! How fortunate we are to have him with us," she cooed.

Cole was not so impressed. He knew the man was only goading him.

"Come," he said to both Miss Deirdre and Nan. "I do believe breakfast is still being served inside the inn."

Nan clapped her hands together. "Oh, Cole, you don't actually mean to say we can linger here for a muffin and perhaps some bacon?"

"Linger we shall," announced Cole, loud enough for Reeve to hear. He felt a moment's satisfaction as the man stiffened, halting momentarily in his tracks. Cole continued. "You may even order your usual kippers, Nan. No request shall be too small this day."

Reeve coughed loudly, turning somewhat to stare in dismay at his lordship.

Cole ignored the reaction. It was high time he took charge of this ridiculous mail run, after all. And what the devil did it matter if he were three hours behind time, or six? As for Miss Marcie needing to be at the inn of Burford posthaste, well, what could he do about it? They were already woefully behind schedule, what with the girl's penchant of saving broken-winged birds, not to mention her unorthodox interest in starving highwaymen! Too, she'd not seemed to give a care when Cole had called out that the coach would depart within the half hour. Indeed, she'd actually ignored his yell.

Imagine that. Cole had never been ignored in his life!

He decided to outwit her. Obviously, she was of a mind to draw out her brief stay at the inn. Well, Cole would do her one better. He had every intention of sitting down to a long and extended breakfast, kippers—if indeed any kippers could be had at the inn—and all. And if Nan or Miss Deirdre felt the urge to rent a room and freshen up a bit, why he would not gainsay them in the least!

Cole smiled to himself, imagining how Miss Marcie would like that.

She wouldn't like it, of course. Not one bit.

And that, Cole realized as he led Miss Deirdre and Nan toward the door, was the only reason he even bothered to enter the inn at all.

Seven

Having an owl perched on one's shoulder made it deuced inconvenient when it came to the matter of finding oneself a table and a seat, Marcie soon learned. The fact that she was much travel-worn and presented herself alone and without chaperone within the inn verily labeled her a milk-and-water miss, one to be noticed and then forgotten just as quickly. The uppity landlord of the establishment took one look at her wrinkled garb and feathered friend and shortly thereafter dismissed her presence entirely.

Marcie found herself jostled about by busy servants and mobcapped chambermaids who rushed to and fro, frantically trying to meet the many needs of the customers. Deciding it best not to make a spectacle of herself by informing the innkeeper of her substantial purse and thus creating an uncomfortable situation for the brusque man, Marcie ducked back outside. She wasn't really that hungry anyway, and a brisk walk round the courtyard would doubtless help clear her head.

She no sooner stepped outside the inn than she espied Cole Coachman, Miss Deirdre on one arm and Nan on the other, heading her way. Nan appeared all agog as she devoured the hectic scene about them. Miss Deirdre, however, had eyes only for Cole Coachman. She bent her golden head toward his, whispering something into his ear.

Cole Coachman, head bent as well, gave a short laugh at whatever it was the woman uttered. Miss Deirdre then tucked her gloved hand deeper into the crook of Cole Coachman's arm. Her eyes verily gleamed with unspoken passion and sultry promises as she gazed up at Cole Coachman's handsome face. In return, the man smiled; it was a knowing smile, meant for one worldly lover from another.

Marcie melted back behind the crowd, pressing her body against the cold boards of the inn exterior. She was startled to realize she was trembling. Her heart beat a queer rhythm, as though she'd just been startled out of her wits—or perhaps had uncovered a glaring and very disturbing truth.

She stayed where she was, hiding behind a tall gentleman, his lady, and their brood. The children were arguing over a peppermint stick.

Cole Coachman, Miss Deirdre clinging to his side, and Nan now trailing a step behind, moved past. They never even noticed Marcie's presence.

Marcie watched them go by, not missing how Cole Coachman gently guided the golden-hued Miss Deirdre inside. Of a sudden, Marcie was glad the insolent innkeeper had denied her a table. She knew without a doubt she would not have been able to bear the sight of her Lord Monarch paying homage to the brazen and very beautiful Miss Deirdre.

Upon entering the establishment, Cole quickly ordered a private parlour to be readied for himself and his traveling companions. The innkeeper, an obnoxious fellow, took one look at Cole and immediately forgot the other patrons.

"My good man, what a pleasure it is to serve you," he enthused.

Cole wasn't fooled by the man's penchant to please. It

was his gold the innkeep was after. Cole Coachman was known along the road to be not only a most accomplished whip but also generous when it came to rewarding those who saw to his comfort.

They were led to a small, cosy parlour where Miss Deirdre immediately divested her comely body of wrap, gloves, and hat, with Cole's help. She expertly guided Cole to the warm hearth, sidling beside him as she made a very pretty show of shivering.

Cole suffered her wily ways only because she was his passenger and because, quite frankly, she was a woman and he was a man. It was not at all a puzzle to Cole why the Regent had deigned to cast his royal eye her way. The woman was very adept at the fine art of seduction.

So why the devil did he continue to wonder about the mischievous Miss Marcie, Cole asked himself. He'd not seen her in the entrance or in the common room. So where could she be?

He hadn't a clue, and as the minutes dragged by, he found himself fretting about her safety. He could only imagine what trouble she'd cast herself into now. Left alone, to her own self, the possibilities were indeed endless.

"Cole, you are daydreaming, I fear," scolded Nan.

Cole brought his mind back to the present. "What's that, Nan?"

"Our breakfast is served, silly. Do sit down and join us, else you'll have Miss Deirdre thinking you are rude."

Cole forced a smile in the general direction of Miss Deirdre. "Forgive me. It has been a long night."

"Why, there is nothing to forgive," said Miss Deirdre. "I cannot imagine how you keep yourself awake for hours on end. But I must admit to you that I have heard murmur of the famous Cole Coachman during my many travels. You seem to have amassed quite a legion of admirers, and now that I've had the pleasure of meeting you, I understand why."

Cole nodded his thanks at her pretty compliment. He pulled out a chair for her, motioning for her to be seated.

Miss Deirdre took that moment to touch her bared hand to his. "Always the supreme gentleman. That is what those along the road say about you . . . among other things," she added, a low, sensuous note in her voice.

Cole knew better than to allow her hand to linger overly long on his. "They are too generous by far," he replied.

Miss Deirdre had the good sense to reach for her napkin once she'd been seated, but as soon as Cole took his own seat to her right, he immediately felt the unmistakable pressure of her silken leg against his.

As Nan made quick work of devouring the varied feast of bacon, eggs, fresh buttermilk, porridge, and even toast and marmalade—there hadn't been a kipper to be found at the inn—Cole was left to deal with the overt attentions of Miss Deirdre. He found his appetite sorely lacking as the woman centered her attention solely upon him.

By the time Nan had eaten the food on her plate, and Miss Deirdre's and Cole's as well, and had downed an unholy amount of tea to boot, Cole realized he could take no more of the prolonged breakfast. He pushed his chair from the table, telling the women he must check on the matter of fresh horses.

Miss Deirdre, sipping at a third cup of tea she'd recently ordered from a harried servant, insisted that he leave the matter to others.

Cole politely reminded her that obtaining the best horses was of extreme importance to a coachman. He did not add that he was, in all actuality, more concerned with the whereabouts of his mischievous Miss Marcie.

"I do so hate for you to go out into the cold," said Miss Deirdre. Her lush mouth formed a perfect pout. She eased back in the chair, allowing Cole full view of her comely shape. "But if you must . . ." Her voice drifted off. She gazed up at him from beneath lazily lidded eyes. "Do you remember that I—and Nan, of course—shall be waiting for you here. Should you decide to come back inside and warm your toes before we again take to the road, I'll not object. Indeed, I'll see to it another warm pot of tea is set in wait for you. And I'll even be certain to move your chair, and mine, closer to the hearth."

She patted the empty seat of his chair, her ungloved fingers smoothing over it as though she were caressing a lover's naked flank.

Cole stared at her, quite mesmerized, and nodded his thanks. But it wasn't Miss Deirdre's beauteous face he saw as he gazed at her. For some confounded reason he kept seeing a pair of flashing green eyes, coupled with a bewitching smile and a wealth of riotous red curls framing a pixie face. Marcie!

Cole cursed himself. Hell and damnation, but the chit was too much on his mind. Imagine, thinking of a runaway schoolgirl when a worldly woman was all but throwing herself at his feet.

Cole turned abruptly on his heel, reached for his greatcoat, hat, and gloves, then departed the parlour, wondering all the while if indeed his heart had become so much mash due to one Marcelon Victoria Darlington.

Rubbish! he told himself sternly. He was simply concerned about the girl. Nothing more. That he kept seeing her face flashing in front of his eyes was testament only to the fact that Miss Marcie had stalked off, alone and unchaperoned. Cole was merely and correctly concerned about her fate. She was, after all, his passenger. And whether he liked it or not—which he didn't, most assuredly—he felt responsible for her safety. God only knew what kind of trouble the girl could create while at this busy inn!

As he stuffed his hat onto his head, jammed his muscled arms into his coat, then forced his gauntlets onto his hands with too much energy, he was suddenly overcome with horrid visions of the mischievous Miss Marcie taking up with all sort of riffraff. The scoundrels of the world would doubtless make a feast of her and then spit her out!

"Bloody hell," Cole muttered to himself as he failed to find Marcie within the busy common room.

He quickened his pace, deepened his search.

She wasn't in the cavernous kitchens; all he found there was several harried maids, a cook who screeched at his interference, and a few plucked geese awaiting the roasting spit.

A further search of the inn turned up nothing more than a lusty lord chasing a willing milkmaid around a scarred table, an abigail and her mistress drying their stockings near a roaring fire, and a snoozing scholar nodding over his books.

There remained only one other parlour to barge into.

Cole, hearing a female scream and the sounds of boots being tossed off and landing on the floor, forced the door open. The latch, severed from its hinges, skittered across the floor as two bemused faces glanced up at him. Cole knew one of those faces as well as he knew his own hand.

"I never expected this from you, of all people!" he said.

"My lor—Cole Coachman!" exclaimed John Reeve, caught as he was in a most compromising position with one of the Cock and Dove's chambermaids.

A mobcapped girl blushed furiously but made no move to cover herself. "Oh, no, John, you'll not be leavin' me side so quick! I've waited near six months to get you here. Stay. Tell your driver to leave us." The chambermaid clutched Reeve's quivering body against her own as she gave Cole a devilish smile. "You'll not be ruinin' our fun, now will you?"

Cole felt a perfect fool.

"Forgive me," he said. "I was looking for someone. I thought I heard her scream."

"Oh, that was me you heard," said the chambermaid. "John here brought me two pretty new bonnets, the finest you ever did see!"

"Forgive me," Cole said again. "I did not mean to—to interrupt." Good God, what an idiot he felt! He tried to back out of the room.

Reeve heaved a huge sigh. "You'll find her in the stables, Cole Coachman."

Cole straightened to his full height. "And how do you know for whom I am searching, Reeve?"

Reeve, giving a quick wink to his most willing partner, turned his face to Cole. "Call it a wild wager." The girl beneath him tugged his attention her way yet again. "She's in the stables, Cole. Now be a good coachman and get on your way, will you?"

Cole turned crimson. The stables! She'd wandered off to the bloody stables? Cole tipped his hat to Reeve.

"My thanks to you, Reeve," he said, stepping back. "Carry on, my good fellow. Carry on."

"That I shall," replied John Reeve.

Cole closed the door, hearing a smothered giggle as he did so. Ah, if only his own life could be so carefree, thought Cole, leaving the lovebirds to their clandestine affair.

But images of Marcie, alone and with no protection, wandering into the stables of the busy inn, filled him with

dread. Visions of ill-usage danced in his brain. God only
knew what scoundrels she would face there. Heavens, but
she could be robbed of what little coin she had. The cut
throats that haunted such establishments would make
game of teasing and toying with her. They would doubtless
take advantage of her youth and inexperience. As for what
such persons would do when they spied her comely shape
and fiery beauty—oh, God, it didn't bear thinking of!

Cole headed for the stables, his heart beating a queer and
unnatural rhythm, and his brain creating a number of odious
scenarios.

He had to find Marcie.

He had to save her, all else be damned!

Marcie leaned back against a warm bale of hay, Prinny
propped on the straw above her, and sized up the pile of
booty she'd amassed during the last roll of Jack the Highwayman's crooked dice.

"I'll see your stolen ruby, and add a necklace of pearls,"
said Marcie, digging out a string of pearls she'd purchased
in London. She wasn't extremely proud of the pearls,
though they were worth a fortune. She'd bought them on a
whim, but only because Mistress Cheltenham had said it
was most unbecoming for a young miss to purchase jewelry
for herself.

Marcie felt a great deal of satisfaction as she dropped
the pearls on the hay-strewn ground.

Ostlers, bootboys, and the few farmboys who'd come to
the inn for some fun, exclaimed over Marcie's wager.

"Mayhap you should take back those pearls, mistress," said
Jack the Highwayman. "They be too fancy for our purses."

"Nonsense," said Marcie. "I wish to wager them, and wager them I shall!"

Jack leaned closer to Marcie. "I wouldn't want to see you be taken advantage of, mistress," he whispered into her ear. "In fact, I've come to like your spunk. Still, I must warn you to take care. Flash pearls like these and someone might choose to stab you in the back."

The other players, overhearing Jack's remark, protested loudly.

"You wound us, Jack my man," said the head ostler. "You wound us with your words as well as with your shaved ivories! We men o' the north don't fancy cheatin'. Now take those queer dice of yours and put 'em back in your pocket!"

Jack looked alarmed.

Marcie laughed. "Oh, Jack, when will you learn you needn't cheat people? We are all just the same, don't you think? I knew you were rolling shaved dice the minute we sat down to play. How do you think I've continued to win such a purse?" So saying, Marcie dumped her winnings down onto the ground. "I say we start anew, and all of us are equal."

Jack cringed, possibly fearing he might be dragged to the magistrate. "I was only trying to see that me horse and I have enough feed to last us through this blasted winter."

"And so you shall, Jack," said Marcie confidently. "Now take my dice, Jack, and see what winning numbers you can roll. They are lucky. You shall see."

Jack took a roll, and much to his amazement, he won. "Well, I'll be!" he exclaimed.

Thirty minutes later all of the gamesters had each amassed a nice pile of winnings. One of the farmboys scooped up Marcie's string of pearls when it was his turn to roll, but Marcie did not mind for she'd won a warm and wooly scarf made of the softest lamb's wool. Jack took in several sugar chunks for his horse, and the head ostler became owner of one shiny silver spoon. Verily, everyone soon agreed that Marcie's ivories were indeed lucky.

One by one they began lifting their battered tins of hot chocolate, taking turns toasting Marcie's pretty lashes, her good health, her smile, and, of course, her lucky dice.

Marcie, thoroughly enjoying herself, made a few toasts of her own. By her third toast, she began to realize the drink had been laced with something headier than chocolate.

"Oh, dear," she murmured. "I dareswear I am beginning to feel a bit light-headed."

"And well you should be, mistress," said Jack. "That chocolate be more rum than anything else. Warms the toes, does it not?"

"Oh, yes!" Marcie giggled, then hiccoughed.

Jack took the tin from her hands. "I do believe you've had more than enough."

"Why, Jack, your concern is touching. Surely, you are not the horrid highwayman you'd hoped us to believe you to be!"

Jack wagged his head. "I did make a blunder of it all, didn't I? Truth be known, mistress, I never stole a thing in all me life, and I'd never pointed me barker at anyone. Sorry I am that I frightened you."

"All is forgiven, Jack . . . but only on one condition."

Jack eyed her closely. "And what might that be, eh?" he asked, suddenly wary.

Marcie leaned close and whispered, "That you'll help me find a way to the inn at Burford. I fear I've angered the great Cole Coachman. No doubt he hopes to be rid of me posthaste. I've done nothing but make him miserable during our ride and so have decided it best not to burden him further with my presence.

"But that does leave me in a perfect pickle, for I've no idea when another coach heading for Burford might come along. And if one does come along, then I fear what might become of me if I travel the distance without a chaperone."

"Say no more!" he said. "Jack here shall find you a seat bound for Burford, and I promise to stick close until you are safely at the inn!"

Marcie blinked. "You would do that for me?"

"That and more. As I see it, mistress, you saved me from the hangman's noose. You done me a good deed. I might be down on me luck, but Jack never forgets a favor. I would be honored to see you safely to your destination."

Marcie smiled. "Oh, Jack, what a perfect gentleman you are. I do believe I have found a friend in you."

The man puffed up with pride, and to Marcie's dismay she noted the glint of tears filling his eyes.

"I never had me a true friend—other than me mum, and a kindly vicar and his wife, who took me in after her death—and surely not one as sweet and beautiful as you be," he said, voice choked.

Marcie reached for his callused hand. She gave it a gentle squeeze. "And I can honestly say that I've never met a man who was so heartstoppingly honest as you have been these minutes past. Honesty becomes you, sir."

Jack blushed furiously. "Yes, well," he muttered, quite flustered. He pulled his hand from hers and yanked a threadbare kerchief from his shabby coat. He quickly mopped at his eyes.

Marcie sat back against the hay bale, feeling both satisfied and a bit weepy herself as she peered at the wide circle of new friends. She hadn't felt this much at home since before her father's death, when she used to ride her pony down to the sea's edge and visit with the fishermen as they readied their boats for a day on the water. It was moments like these that she'd sorely missed while being cooped up in Mistress Cheltenham's drafty attic.

One of the ostlers drew out a harmonica and began to play a lively tune. The youngest farmboy whittled away at some wood, his knife blade moving to the tune. Two of the bootboys joined an errant kitchen maid, who had stolen inside the stables with yet another pitcher of the potent hot chocolate and a loaf of steaming bread as well, in the middle of the stable. The three commenced to dance a jig.

Marcie clapped her hands and laughed as the bootboys took turns twirling the comely lass about. Before Marcie knew it, she too was pulled into the merriment.

"Oh, no," said Marcie, shaking her head. She shyly pulled away. "I cannot! What I mean to say is, I—I don't know how to dance."

Jack moved beside her. "A pretty miss such as yourself was never taught to dance?" he exclaimed. "Pity, that! But never fear, Jack here shall learn you a few steps."

"You?" Marcie said, quite surprised.

Jack winked. "Me mum might not have had the blunt to keep me belly full, but she had the lightest feet in all the north, she did. I learned to dance just as soon as I learned to walk. Here now, you just follow me lead, mistress."

Marcie, her eyes aglow in anticipation, did indeed follow Jack's lead, and all too soon she gave herself over to the wild elation within her. Ah, to have someone actually teach her how to dance! Famous!

She swirled about the floor, her bonnet cast aside, and her fiery curls in riotous disarray about her flushed face.

The ostlers stomped their feet, hands clapping. Horses nickered, coming awake with the music and laughter.

Round and round Marcie went, spirits soaring. Oh, how she'd dreamed of being allowed to dance while in London, but Mistress Cheltenham had forbidden Marcie from joining in any of the fun, and truth be known, Marcie had not wanted to learn to dance with any of her uppish schoolmates, knowing they would ridicule her awkward steps.

But this was different. Here, in this cosy stable, Marcie could be anything she wanted to be. She could trip over her own feet—which she did, many times—and no one batted an eyelash. They merely laughed along with her, encouraging her to dance some more. And dance she did. She danced until the pins tumbled out of her hair, and her cheeks grew hot, and her eyes sparkled.

One of the bootboys, just as much caught up in the excitement, took hold of her hands and spun her round so hard and so fast that Marcie was sent spinning out of control. She whirled right into Jack's arms. They collided with great speed, tumbling head over heels into a stray bale of hay. Marcie let out a scream of delight.

It was then Cole Coachman came charging into the stable. A fire-breathing devil he appeared. He took one look at Marcie lying in a heap in the hay, and immediately charged toward Jack.

"Unhand her, you scoundrel!" bellowed Cole Coachman.

Marcie sat up on her elbows, blowing a red curl from her eyes. "Cole, no!" she cried, realizing his intent. "Jack did me no harm! He—"

But she was too late.

Cole Coachman yanked Jack to his feet, then, just as quickly, delivered a clean punch to the man's whiskered jaw.

Jack fell back, out cold.

Eight

Cole certainly hadn't intended to resort to fisticuffs like some baseborn fool, but both pride and good breeding fell to the wayside the minute he'd found Marcie being mauled in a hay bale by some thieving highwayman.

Seeing her caught beneath the man's bulk, her hair in wild confusion and her skirts hitched up and showing a shocking amount of trim ankle caused Cole's blood to boil, and his indignation to mount to terrifying heights. How dare anyone lay a hand on his Mistress Mischief?

"Get to your feet and face me man to man!" Cole said in a murderous tone. "I am far from finished with teaching you a lesson you'll not soon forget."

A horrid hush filled the stable as the highwayman failed to move. Indeed, every person present stood stock-still, scarcely breathing and waiting to see what would transpire.

Everyone but Marcie.

"Save your breath, you odious coachman!" Marcie snapped at Cole. "My friend isn't about to be standing up to you anytime soon, nor anyone else for that matter. You've knocked him senseless, you have, and for naught!"

Cole gaped at the too lovely Miss Marcie. "For naught?" he sputtered. *"For naught?"*

"That is exactly what I said. Have you lost your hearing as well as your good sense?"

Quite thunderstruck, Cole watched as Marcie gingerly wriggled her way from beneath Jack's solid form. That done, she made no motion to scoot away from him as Cole had expected her to do, since by all appearances the man had been mistreating her.

Rather, she unwrapped a much-worn scarf from about her neck, a scarf she'd somehow obtained since Cole had last seen her, then cradled the man's head upon it. She gently patted the man's weathered cheek, trying to rouse him with both her soft touch and a few whispered words.

A small-framed youth broke free of the circle of bystanders behind Cole. He scurried past Cole with frightened haste, then kneeled beside Miss Marcie.

"He dead?" the boy asked.

"I should hope not," said Marcie, shooting an angry scowl in the general direction of Cole.

Cole watched in dismay as the others soon crowded round the lovely miss and her fallen highwayman. One by one they crouched down beside the two, all of them holding vigil over the threadbare thief.

Cole felt very much the villain. And to think, not a minute ago, he'd come raging into the stable, imagining himself to be the white knight rushing to his damsel's rescue. This damsel obviously needed no rescue. It was on the tip of Cole's tongue to utter an apology of sorts, but Jack took that moment to come round.

"What hit me?" he muttered.

Cole felt the weight of too many eyes upon him. For the very first time in his life, he wished the earth would open up and swallow him into its dark, dank depths.

Miss Marcie turned her attention back to the highwayman. "I fear it was our own Cole Coachman. He did not break your jaw, did he, my friend?"

The highwayman had the good humor to smile. "Naw. Me jaw is as sturdy as a tree trunk, mistress."

Cole heard her sigh of relief, a sound which managed to cause him much discomfort. So she'd come to care for the highwayman, had she? Was now addressing him as "my friend," was she? Now how the devil had that come about? Cole felt an unexpected prick of pain pierce the nether regions of his hard heart.

"Perhaps we should summon a physician," said one of the men crouched about Jack.

The highwayman shook his head, winced, then replied, "No need . . . that is, if yonder coachman isn't set on making mincemeat of me body."

Again, too many accusing eyes turned toward Cole.

Cole straightened, quelling the urge to flex the fingers of his right hand; Jack's jaw had been monstrous solid. He cleared his throat. "I see no need for further confrontation. It has become quite obvious to me that I misjudged the situation. I had thought Miss Marcie was in trouble. Clearly, I was wrong," he announced.

Jack gave a crooked grin up at Cole. "No need to apologize, Cole Coachman. As I figure it, you had every right to cut me down to size seeing as how I waylaid your coach and all. Truth be known, I feel a world better now that you've taken a swing at me. As I see it, we're even as even can be, eh?"

Cole quelled the urge to haul the slippery thief to his feet and knock him down yet again. Even indeed.

Feeling outnumbered, though, he held his tongue—and stayed his temper. What mattered most to Cole at the moment was regaining Marcie's trust. He'd made a perfect idiot of himself in her eyes, no doubt. She must think him an uncouth beast.

To Marcie, he said, "Our coach leaves for Burford within the quarter hour. If you return to the inn, you'll find Nan and Miss Deirdre relaxing in a private parlour. You'll find some food there as well."

Marcie turned her face away from him. "I am not hungry," she said. "I've decided to stay here, with my friends."

"Surely you cannot be serious!"

"And why not?" she brazenly challenged.

Damn, thought Cole, but she could be a mulish miss! Too bad for him that she'd quite enraptured him with her mischievous ways and quicksilver moods.

She looked a perfect hoyden with her hair all atumble and her eyes bright with passion. Since she had relieved herself of her fur-lined pelisse, Cole found himself viewing the full luster of her charms. She was not the too-thin runaway he'd first imagined. Indeed, her comely curves were very much in evidence beneath her pretty gown. Her bosom heaved with righteous indignation, and Cole found himself remembering all too clearly the sight of her lovely ankles, shown to great advantage just moments ago.

It wouldn't do at all for him to become doe-eyed now, thought Cole sternly. He must hold his meandering thoughts in check. She was his passenger, and like it or not, his responsibility. He couldn't very well allow her her own head and leave her to this mishmash of "friends" she thought she'd found.

"You told me yourself you wish to arrive at the inn of Burford, posthaste," he said.

"And so I shall," replied Miss Marcie. "Jack has promised to see me safely to the inn."

"Oh, he has, has he?"

"Yes," said Miss Marcie, a bit too defiant.

Cole's jaw tightened. God's teeth, but the girl needed a strict rein.

One young lad mustered the wherewithal to stand up and face Cole. "We were just having a bit o' fun, Cole Coachman. The mistress taught us all how to roll her lucky ivories. Why, I even won me a strand of pearls. And Jack, he won some sugar fer his tired nag. And then, well, we all got a mite carried away with our winnings, and soon we were dancing a jig. Miss Marcie dances the best jig I ever did see! But I got to spinning her too fast and before I knew it she was tumbling down into the hay. Jack only tried to soften her fall, he did. That's all there was to it. Just a dance. Nothing more."

Cole didn't know whether to smile or be outraged. His Mistress Mischief had been gambling and dancing . . . in a stable, no less. Good Lord. Had he saved her from a stuffy school only to cast her into an even worse scenario? And now the chit thought to stay on at the inn and allow the highwayman to transport her "safely" to Burford.

Unbelievable.

Cole fought hard to contain his temper, as well as his feelings of guilt. For all he knew, the girl would sprint off with Jack and soon become mistress to a highwayman!

"Miss Marcie," said Cole, his voice clipped, "I would have a word with you. Alone."

Marcie lifted her chin. "I see no need—"

"Now," said Cole, moving forward and reaching for her.

The runaway schoolgirl had no choice but to do as he asked. She left Jack to the ministrations of the others as Cole verily dragged her into the center of the stable.

"Ouch!" she cried. "You are pinching my wrist!"

"Forgive me," said Cole, "but yet again your antics have sorely tested my patience. I dareswear your father would roll over in his grave should he know you've taken up gambling in a stable."

"And I daresay my father would be most sorely vexed should he know you knocked a poor, defenseless man silly only because he dared save me from a nasty fall!"

"What I should have done upon meeting your highwayman was drag him to the nearest magistrate, my fine filly!"

"I am not 'your' anything," Marcie shot back. "Nor is Jack 'my' highwayman!"

"Then why the deuce do you continue fussing over his welfare?"

"Would you have preferred I left him to rot on the floorboards?"

Yes, thought Cole. Anything would have been preferable to seeing his Mistress Mischief fawning over the shabby man.

"He is naught but a thief, and a sorry one at that," Cole said.

"And there you err," said Marcie. "He is my friend. He has not cast judgment on me merely because I've chosen to secret myself away from an odious boarding school. Indeed, Jack has been kind enough to assure me that he'll remain by my side until I make my way to Burford. He has promised to deliver me safely to my destination and has not once chastised me. Unlike you, Cole Coachman, Jack has proved to be nothing short of a gentleman!"

Cole scowled. "If that shifty man appears a gentleman in your eyes, then I cease to wonder why the mistress of your boarding school locked you in an attic. No doubt it was to save you from your own self!"

Those were the wrong words to say, obviously, for there came the sudden glint of wetness in Marcie's bewitching green eyes.

"Oh, bother—you are not going to cry, are you?" Cole demanded, trying to maintain control over his own roiling emotions. Why was it he kept saying and doing all the wrong things where Marcie was concerned?

She lifted her pretty chin, stalwart defiance chasing the sadness from her eyes. "Certainly not!" she said. "Tears are—are quite a useless reaction, I've learned." She mopped hastily at her damp eyes. "Do be assured I don't give a . . . a damn what conclusions you've arrived at concerning me, Cole Coachman! You should doubtless be relieved to know that I shall no longer have the chance to waylay your precious run. Now if you'll excuse me. . . ."

She made a motion to turn away from him.

Something in Cole snapped. He reached for her hand. "Don't," he whispered. "Don't do this."

Perhaps Marcie's tears forced him to stay her. Perhaps it was his own cold heart thawing just a little at her tenderness that made him reach out to her. Whatever it was, Cole found himself taking her hand in his.

He cleared his suddenly tight throat. "I—I wish to be the one to see you safely to Burford," he blurted.

The wariness in her eyes proved pure torture.

"Why?" she whispered.

Why indeed? thought Cole. But he knew why. It was because he couldn't tolerate saying farewell to her just now, because he couldn't fathom climbing back onto his cold bench, alone, and knowing he might never see her again.

Cole found he couldn't form the words that were truly in his heart. He couldn't blurt out that he'd actually come to care for her in some odd, too-forceful kind of way. No. He couldn't say those things. The Marquis of Sherringham wasn't known for wearing his heart on his sleeve. Just the opposite.

"Because I don't fancy standing idly by while you whistle your reputation down the wind," he said instead, a bit too brusquely for his own comfort. "No proper young lady would enlist the aid of a highwayman to see her safely to her destination. You must realize that a proper miss wouldn't set out on the open road with a highwayman!"

At that, the fight drained out of her. Her comely shoulders slumped. She pressed her eyes shut tight, bowed her head. "You are right," she whispered, the words almost inaudible.

Hesitantly, Cole asked, "So you'll allow me to take you to Burford?" A moment of silence slid past, time enough for Cole to wonder if he'd been too harsh.

"Yes," she finally whispered. "I shall travel with you."

Cole released a long-held breath of air he wasn't aware he'd been holding.

"But," said Marcie, lifting her head, and her mood suddenly turning light, "only if Jack can join us."

"Oh for the love of—fine, fine," he muttered, not at all happy, but realizing Miss Marcie wouldn't budge an inch if he denied her request. "Jack may come along. But if he makes any move to rob us blind, I'll see him strung up by his toes!"

Miss Marcie smiled. "He'll not be strung up anywhere lest I be strung up beside him."

"You are that fond of the man?" Cole asked, dismayed.

Marcie flashed him a winning smile. "Until I met Jack," she said honestly, "no one ever thought to teach me how to dance." With that, she moved away from him, heading for her highwayman and stable friends.

Cole watched her go, and for the merest moment allowed himself to imagine himself and Marcie in the grand ballroom

of Sherringham House. Oh, he could teach her to dance . . .
and more.

It was the yearning to teach her "more" that troubled
him.

Nine

True to Cole Coachman's words, they left the inn within the quarter hour, but Marcie did not warm the bench beside him—Miss Deirdre did. And rather prettily, too, Marcie conceded upon leaving the stable and spying the worldly woman perched provocatively upon the hard wood. Snuggled in several layers of fur rugs, her golden hair hidden beneath a warm and stylish bonnet, and her long, slender fingers gloved in the finest kid skin, she looked like a queen—a decidedly sultry one, but a queen nonetheless.

She waved a cheery good morning to Marcie, calling out that she wished to give her a rest from the biting chill and so had abandoned her seat inside the coach.

"No need to thank me, sweet child," she said as Marcie stared up at her. "You must have been frozen stiff riding atop this horrid bench all through the night. Never fear. You may take my seat inside. I shall keep our fine coachman company. Indeed, I am often up with the sun—shocking though that habit may be—and do admit to enjoying the brisk morning air."

Marcie sincerely doubted such a thing, but she wasn't about to call more attention to herself by arguing with the woman. What did she care if the lady wished to freeze her toes and her nose alongside the grumpy Cole Coachman?

Marcie wished Miss Deirdre a comfortable ride, knowing

by experience the lady would be most *un*comfortable, and headed for the carriage door, Prinny atop her right shoulder.

Jack scurried to help her inside. "Here, mistress. Allow me."

Nan was already well established within the coach.

"Thank you, Jack, but truly you needn't fuss over me. I am just glad you agreed to join me on my way to Burford."

Jack nodded even as he craned his neck to get a better view of Miss Deirdre, who'd taken to stretching like a sleepy kitten. "Lor' " he whispered, awestruck. "I'll be . . ."

"You'll be what?" Marcie asked testily, knowing very well where his gaze and thoughts had wandered. She tugged hard at his sleeve.

Jack absently let down the steps, which crashed down on Marcie's booted toes.

"Jack!" cried Marcie.

"Eh? Oh, sorry," he muttered. He shook himself to attention, realigned the steps, then made a grand show of helping Marcie into the carriage. "I be daydreaming," he said guiltily.

"I gathered as much. Doubtless your daydreams are filled with visions of Miss Deirdre."

"Ah, she be a beauteous angel, if I ever did see one."

Gracious, thought Marcie, *but must every male trip over his tongue at the mere sight of the wily Miss Deirdre?*

"She is but a woman, Jack," Marcie reminded the man. "No angel. Not by far, I suspect."

"Close enough," Jack said. Clearly smitten, he straightened to his not-so-threatening height, whipped off his filthy hat, and dragged his fingers through his unkempt hair. "She be travelling with us to Burford?" he asked.

"Yes," replied Marcie. *Unfortunately,* she thought.

Jack beamed, preening like a peacock. "Will wonders

never cease? Not only have I found me a true friend in you, but along comes the bright beauty of me dreams. I be doubly blessed this fine morn."

"Jack, surely you cannot believe yourself in love with that . . . that creature."

"I can, and I am."

"But you've not even met her!"

"Love works in a queer fashion, to be sure, mistress. I don't need to meet her, just see her. She be the woman for Jack, make no mistake about it. After all," he added, winking, "it is Saint Valentine's Day, y'know. A day for love . . . and for lovers."

Marcie didn't need to be reminded of the date. She'd not forgotten about the holiday, about sweet Valentines and precious verses she'd not be receiving. Nor did she bother to inform the highwayman that Miss Deirdre would as like as not turn her prettily shaped nose up at him. The woman clearly was one accustomed to the finer things in life. Too, it was obvious her taste in men leaned toward those who could afford to keep her in grand style . . . and perhaps toward such rugged, moody types as Cole Coachman.

This last thought did not sit well with Marcie. She didn't like being forced to take a seat inside the coach when only hours before she'd been just as forced to join Cole on his bench. But climb inside she did.

Jack poked his head inside the carriage long enough to see that Marcie had ample space to recline. He gave her a wink, promising he would keep a sharp eye on any fellow thieves haunting the roads.

"I be the perfect one to ferret out any scoundrels set to raiding this coach. Rest assured, I'll see you safely arrive at your destination, mistress."

Marcie thanked him, breathing a sigh of relief when he

finally shut the door. She leaned back against the squabs, blowing out another breath of air.

Nan, with bandboxes and presents again piled on either side of her, cooed in delight. "Marcie, I do think you've quite captured the man's interest. How dashing! Imagine, dancing with a *highwayman*," she said with delicious glee. "Cole told us all about your highwayman. Said you'd become oddly fond of the scoundrel."

Marcie frowned. "Jack isn't a scoundrel, Nan. He was just down on his luck. As it happens, ours was the first coach he ever attempted to rob."

"Still," said Nan, excited, "he is a highwayman. And you did defend him. That's what Cole says, anyway. He warned me and Miss Deirdre away from the man. Said we'd be getting in over our pretty heads if we allowed the man to try and sway us with his forked tongue."

"Fustian," said Marcie. "Pure and utter fustian."

"So you *are* enamored of the highwayman. No wonder Cole has become a perfect crosspatch. He's quite put out that you've taken a fancy to Jack. No doubt he is just eaten with jealousy. He was shooting fire from his nostrils when he came to collect us from the parlour. Mumbled some such thing about you rolling ivories with a band of miscreants. How delicious! And to think you'd only intended to flee from Mistress Cheltenham's stuffy school. Oh, Marcie, but you seem to be enjoying the lark of your life! Is this not grand fun, this ride?"

Marcie frowned. "This is not 'the lark of my life,' Nan. Hardly that. It has been a perfectly horrible time and—" Marcie stopped short. "What did you just say? About Cole Coachman, that is."

"I said he was spitting fire when—"

"Not *that*," said Marcie impatiently. Cole was forever spitting fire when it came to her. She knew that much. "You said something about . . . about jealousy," she said, her heart seemingly fearing to beat until she'd heard the words again.

"Oh, he's as jealous as jealous can be, make no mistake about that," replied Nan. "Why, I do believe, he is a bit smitten with you, Marcie. I declare Cole has never been preoccupied with a female as he has been this past hour with you."

Marcie's heart gave a wild kick. She studiously tried to control its odd flutter, but to no avail. Cole Coachman smitten with her? Preposterous! He was vexed with her, nothing more.

And yet, the mere possibility of the handsome coachman harboring warm thoughts about her made Marcie's heart soar into her throat.

"Marcie?" said Nan, eyeing her friend. "Whatever is the matter? You are blushing furiously. *Oh!* Do not say that you have taken a fancy to Cole!"

"Certainly not," Marcie said. "And I am *not* blushing. I—I am just overheated."

"In this frigid air? Go on with you. You rather like the idea of Cole's being jealous of you and your highwayman. Tell me true now. You like it, you do!"

"Nan! Enough of this talk. I—I am not about to lose my heart."

"And why ever not?" asked Nan. " 'Tis the perfect season for losing one's heart. How romantic to fall in love on the morn of Saint Valentine's Day! And Cole Coachman is such a fine catch, Marcie, to be sure."

Marcie frowned. "He is a coachman who, as you once hinted, has the women tripping over their feet to get near him."

"I did say something like that," Nan agreed, adding slyly,

"but I never said Cole ever took a fancy to one of them. Until now, that is. You must admit he seems a mite too concerned about your welfare, Marcie."

"But only because he whisked me from the mews of Mistress Cheltenham's horrid school. Doubtless he feels responsible for my safety. Nothing more."

"Pshaw!" Nan waved one hand in the air. "If he were worried about seeing a runaway schoolgirl to safety, he would have set you off at the first post with stern orders for you to be transported back to your home in Cornwall. Believe me, Marcie, Cole is not a man to burden himself with a tag-along miss. He just isn't the sort to take too many under his protective wing."

"No? Then why has he taken such pains to see to Miss Deirdre's welfare?" Marcie found herself shamelessly asking.

"The answer to that is easy enough, I dareswear. Miss Deirdre is hardly a runaway schoolgirl, as you must know," replied Nan. She leaned forward on her seat, whispering conspiratorially, "But what you probably don't realize is that Miss Deirdre is . . . well, she is, ah . . . how to put this?"

"Just spit it out, Nan. What the deuce is Miss Deirdre, exactly?"

Nan shivered with gossipy glee. "She's none other than the Regent's latest lover!"

Marcie gasped.

"It's true, I swear! She told me so herself but swore me to secrecy. Now don't you go spreading this tale, for it is for your ears and yours alone."

"And who would I tell, Nan? You and I both know I don't move in any lofty circles."

"But you could," said Nan truthfully. "Your beauty alone could see you there, not to mention the tidy inheritance bequeathed to you by your doting father. La, Marcie, but I do declare you could become one of Prinny's conquests, or perhaps be squired about on the arm of a peer!"

Marcie shuddered with disgust. "Perish the thought. I've no desire to bump elbows with any member of the ton."

Nan's eyes twinkled with devilry. "Not even if you met a handsome, titled swell who had the power to sweep you off your feet?"

"Not even," Marcie said. "The lot of them are too top-lofty, by far. And stuffy, so I've heard. I prefer not to meet any of them."

"And do you also prefer to become a spinster?"

Marcie wrinkled her pert nose. "I am hardly on the shelf."

"But you will be if you don't soon take an interest in some man," Nan pointed out. "Why shouldn't you consider Cole's attentions? A match between yourself and this coachman would not be so awful, would it? You've enough gold to keep the both of you—and generations of your offspring—in grand style. Surely, if you can pair yourself with a slippery thief, you can just as easily set your sights on a fine coachman."

"Egad!" Marcie cried. "I've hardly paired myself with Jack, Nan. He has become a friend, nothing more. As for setting my cap at Cole Coachman . . . well, don't be ridiculous. The man loathes me. Any passerby could ascertain that fact. And—and besides," she added a bit too forcefully, "I find him far too arrogant and moody for my tastes. He is forever blowing hot and cold."

"But only because you obviously drive him to distraction," said Nan.

Marcie clicked her tongue. "You are too dramatic by far. And a helpless romantic, to boot."

"Am I now?" said Nan, snuggling deeper between the

mountain of packages on either side of her. "Perhaps I am the only one with a clear view of the situation. Love, after all, can be a tricky thing." Nan then yawned, closed her eyes, and without so much as an apology for ending the conversation so abruptly, fell fast asleep.

Marcie stared at her friend. How the devil the girl could sleep with the jostling motion of the coach was quite beyond Marcie's grasp. Too, Nan's talk of love being a tricky thing reminded Marcie of what Jack had said. The opinions of her friends appeared to be that love could—and would—steal over one with no warning whatsoever.

Marcie turned her face toward the window of the coach and steadied her gaze on the winter landscape breezing past. She frowned. Had she fallen in love with Cole Coachman? Was that the reason she was so bothered by the man?

"Fustian," she muttered to herself. How could she be in love with a man she barely knew?

And why, oh why, was she so deuced interested in whether or not Cole fussed over her welfare only because she was his passenger or because he'd actually taken a personal interest in her?

And more to the point, what was Cole's interest in the lovely Miss Deirdre, purported lover to none other than Prinny himself?

Marcie spent the next several hours contemplating such intricate questions. In fact, she was so caught up in her musings that she did not bother to alight from the coach when Cole Coachman made yet another quick stop to unload a few more parcels and secure a fresh team of horses. She was not at all pleased that memories of Cole—holding her in his warm and muscled embrace, of him sharing with her some ginger root, and of him raging into the stables only to land a fist on Jack's sturdy jaw—kept invading her mind. And no matter how hard she tried, she couldn't banish the coachman's stormy gray eyes from her thoughts.

"Oh bloody hell," she whispered, using one of Cole Coachman's favored phrases. "Have I truly fallen in love with the man?"

And as though to haunt her, both Jack's and Nan's theories on love came crashing into her thoughts. If this was love, it was indeed queer. And it had indeed swept Marcie off her feet.

She sighed, watching the snowflakes fall past the window. Drowsy at last, she vaguely ascertained that the Royal Mail coach was heading into the eye of another winter storm. As for herself, she realized, perhaps a shade too late, that her heart was tumbling fast into a maelstrom of passion that began and ended with the enigmatic Cole Coachman. . . .

Cole swore under his breath as he charged his team into a wall of whipping snow. Gadzooks, but the weather had taken a turn for the worse. A blizzard, that's what it was.

"Hell and damnation," Cole muttered, as he guided his horses straight into the seemingly impenetrable wall of falling snow. He could barely see his own gloved hands, let alone the road.

"Wh—what's th—that y—you s—say?" queried Miss Deirdre, shivering beside him on the bench. Her teeth clacked together, a most unpleasant sound.

Cole frowned. He should have stopped long ago and insisted she climb inside the carriage to find some warmth. But he'd been plagued by visions of Miss Marcie these many miles past and had been hard pressed to keep his mind and his wits about him.

For the life of him he couldn't get thoughts of Marcie

out of his mind. He saw her wherever he looked. He saw her scurrying out of the snowy mews in Town, looking frightened but purposeful as she'd stepped into his path; saw her crumble atop the snow, sick from too many bonbons; and recalled her, finally, all atumble in the hay of a stable, skirts hitched up and showing her pretty ankles, burnished curls framing her pixie face, and her eyes so bright and filled with merriment . . .

Lord, but she'd be the death of him yet! thought Cole, as he urged his team around another tricky bend in the road. Unfortunately, an abandoned farm cart, buried in the snow, sat directly in their path.

"Whoa!" Cole shouted, pulling hard on the reins.

The horses snorted, frightened into panic. They bounded to the side, limbs flailing as they made a great show of avoiding the farm cart. Cole had no choice but to give them their head and allow them to veer straight for a drift of deep snow.

Miss Deirdre screamed. Cole cursed. In a split second, the team heaved the coach deep into a crusty bank of snow. And there the coach bottomed out, firmly embedding itself in an ice-encrusted mound of chalky white. The horses blew out steams of breath, as they floundered in the snow trying to find some sure footing. The Mail coach was truly and utterly stuck.

Cole dropped the reins. Miss Deirdre, teeth still chattering, muttered about having broken a fingernail in all the commotion. John Reeve came bounding off the hind boot, complaining that now he and he alone would be forced to unhitch one of the leaders and head for the next Mail post without any assistance.

Cole would have given them all over to the devil at that moment. Imagine! Having landed his coach in a snowbank!

His fellow peers in the Whip Driving Club would doubtless roll with laughter at such a thing. Clearly, he'd been so obsessed with thoughts of Miss Marcie that he'd not been thinking straight.

"Whatever shall we do?" cried Miss Deirdre, quite unhinged by this nasty turn of events.

"Why, you walk, that's what," supplied John Reeve, even now heading toward his mail bags.

"Walk?" exclaimed Miss Deirdre, a telling terror in her voice. "But to *where?"*

"To the nearest farmhouse," Reeve answered.

Miss Deirdre nearly fainted.

Cole cursed the guard for worrying the woman. "All is not lost," Cole said in an attempt to soothe her. He jumped down from the bench, ascertained the damage, then added, "Perhaps I can guide the horses and have them pull the coach free."

"Impossible," said Reeve. "You're stuck, my lor—Cole Coachman. I suggest you and the passengers should get your feet moving and not even try to free this coach." Reeve, grumbling like a bear, pulled Cole out of hearing distance from the coach, and in a low voice growled, "Can't say as I didn't warn you not to take on this run, my lord. If you were truly a coachman, I'd box your ears for the mess you've made of this!"

"Now see here," Cole began, quite affronted.

But Reeve would have none of it. "No, 'tis high time you listened to me—that is, begging your pardon, my lord," he added hastily. "But you've got me in a fix, you have. As Mail guard, I am sworn to a twelve-nour duty, from beginning to end of this run. By my calculations, I am now long past my end of duty, yet I've miles to go before I reach my final post. Had the usual coachman been at the reins of this coach he'd have been off-duty hours ago and I'd be propping my feet before a warm hearth."

Cole could not argue the fact that he had indeed made a mess of this Mail run. All in all, it was both unusual and outrageous.

"You are absolutely in the right, my good man," said Cole, properly brought down to size. "Rest assured I shall give a glowing report to your Post Office. Your employer and fellow guards shall learn of your devoted service. In fact, I shall personally see to it a letter of commendation is writ on your behalf."

Reeve's anger dissipated in the face of such a fine apology. "You are too kind, my lor—Cole Coachman," Reeve replied, sufficiently pacified. "I am sorry if I've been gruff with you, but surely you must understand how it is. After all, it ain't every day a swell takes the reins of a coach I am hired to guard."

"I understand, Reeve. No need to apologize, not when we both know that I am to blame for all the trouble we've encountered along the road."

Reeve grinned. "Seems to me all our trouble started the minute Miss Marcie climbed on board. Now mind you, I'm not complaining. She is a sweet thing. And lovely, too. Perhaps too lovely, eh?" Reeve leaned closer, adding softly, "Guard her well, my lord, for I do believe she is just your cup of tea. Lively as the day is long, but a true lady underneath all her spunk. Perhaps the good Lord knew what He was doing when He sent her running into your path from the snowy mews, eh?"

With that, John Reeve reached for his letter bag, making certain the way-bill, containing all details of passengers, parcels, and luggage, was secured safely within it. He swung the heavy bag over one shoulder, then headed to unhitch a horse.

Cole followed after him, watching as the man made haste to mount the beast.

Once in the saddle, Reeve tipped his hat. "I shall report your disaster at the next post. Take care of our passengers, I pray, and do you take my advice concerning your runaway school miss," he added softly.

Cole smiled. "Godspeed, John Reeve. And a happy Saint Valentine's Day to you."

"And to you, my lor—Cole Coachman," Reeve corrected hastily.

Cole laughed.

Reeve laughed as well, and then he rode away, snow spitting from beneath his mount's hooves.

Cole turned his attention to his remaining horses, and his passengers.

Jack was surveying the scene with a critical eye. "Yup," he surmised. "We be stuck. Can't say as I didn't expect as much, what with all the snow."

"Dash it," said Cole, not wanting to hear the man's voice, let alone view his wily face. Indeed, every time Cole looked at Jack, he inevitably thought of Miss Marcie and how she'd enjoyed dancing with the man.

It did not sit well that Cole—very much viewed to be a fine 'catch' of the ton, and whispered to be supremely light of feet while on the dance floor—had no way of proving to Miss Marcie that he was by far more of a gentleman than Jack could ever dream of being.

Jack, however, puffed up with pride as he opened the coach door and dropped down the steps, encouraging both Nan and Miss Marcie to climb down.

"We be stuck, me lovely ladies," he said. "But never fear.

Jack, here, shall lead you to safety. Why, I combed these very lands as a young lad, and I know of a certain vicar and his wife who will take us in without question. No doubt they'll set us up in grand style."

A sleepy Nan, followed by a concerned Marcie, Prinny the owl perched on her shoulder, climbed out of the coach. Jack immediately moved to help Miss Deirdre down from the box as Cole tried to calm his horses. In no time at all, Jack won the trust of Cole's female passengers. And too soon, all of them were blindly following Jack onto a snowy path.

"Do be quick there, mate," carolled Jack over one shoulder to Cole.

Cole, left alone with the horses, cursed the thief. No doubt the man would see them all spending the day in a drafty, decrepit barn. And why the deuce, Cole wondered, did Marcie so willingly trust the thief?

Cole swore under his breath. He unhitched the three remaining horses and fought to keep the beasts in line as he hurried to catch up with the highwayman. Cole decided he was a perfect widgeon for following Jack's lead. But follow he did, for he had no choice.

As Cole trudged after the others, he soon admitted to himself that he would follow Marcie to the ends of the earth, and beyond.

But it wasn't love for the girl that spurred him, he told himself sternly. It couldn't be. She was but a runaway school miss. And he, well, he was Lord Sherringham, jaded and cold, and decidedly fastidious. It wouldn't do at all for his lordship to become smitten with an errant, mulish miss. The girl was simply a thorn in his side. Nothing more. Once she reached her destination, Cole would be free of any obligation toward her. He could finally tell her good-bye, thought he.

Or could he?

Ten

The heavily falling snow soon lessened, becoming a dreamy view of huge, fluffy flakes drifting lazily from the sky. Marcie, following the trio of Nan, Jack, and Miss Deirdre into a thick copse laden with snow, could not help but glance over her shoulder, concerned about the ever-moody Cole Coachman. She caught a glimpse of his tall form amidst the falling whiteness just before she rounded a curve in the path. How handsome he looked with his hat cocked back on his dark-haired head, his strong, aquiline features caught in concentration as he expertly guided his horses through the deep snow.

Marcie paused only a moment, drinking in the sight of him as he bent to whisper some unheard words to the lead horse. A lock of his dark hair tumbled in romantic fashion onto his forehead, and Marcie found herself wishing ridiculously that she might be nearer to him—both physically and emotionally—so that she could brush that lone lock back into place.

"Oh, fiddlesticks," she grumbled to herself. What a foolish chit she was being in harboring such a thought.

Surely the man would not be pleased to know she was thinking about him, Marcie decided. Indeed, he would most likely heave a sigh of relief should she simply disappear from his life altogether! Had it not been for her, Cole

Coachman would have finished his run hours ago, and would doubtless have raced ahead of the snowstorm that now left his coach buried in a snowdrift.

Marcie felt uncommonly guilty. She'd never intended to create such a coil for the man, and yet she had done nothing less than exactly that. Oh, bother, but she managed to completely foul his plans with her wild lark of running away from her boarding school. She must somehow make amends to the man.

Marcie pulled her gaze away from Cole Coachman. She hurried to catch up with the others, all the while trying to think of a way to help brighten Cole Coachman's day. Surely there must be something she could do that would bring a smile to his lips.

Several minutes later, Jack led the women to their destination. Marcie nearly cried with delight when she broke free from the wintry copse and saw a large and rambling vicarage.

"What a beautiful place you've led us to, Jack!" she exclaimed.

"It be heaven on earth," breathed Jack, a bit misty-eyed at seeing the place that was as peaceful-looking as his childhood memory painted it as being. "Vicar Clarke and his wife be ever so pleasant. They be known for taking in orphans and the like, so be forewarned when I say we might be met with much fuss and confusion."

"Lovely," whispered Marcie. "A perfect welcome on such a snowy Saint Valentine's Day."

She ran ahead of the others then, letting herself skip over a snow-covered footbridge that held the recent imprint of many little feet.

A yapping sheepdog met her at the low stone wall that encompassed the immediate grounds. Prinny ruffled his feathers in alarm, but Marcie quickly soothed him with a soft voice, then set him on the wall, out of reach of the dog. That done, Marcie thought nothing of bending down to scratch the dog behind its thick ears. The old dog beat its tail against her skirts, diving his nose into the crook of her arm.

"I'll be," murmured Jack, coming up behind Marcie. "If it ain't old Bart. Thought he'd be dead by now."

"I daresay he's quite alive," said Marcie.

She laughed as the dog took one sniff of Jack's leg, then bounded up to plant his forelegs on the man's chest, giving a great slap of his tongue to Jack's weathered cheek.

Jack grinned from ear to ear. "Bart, me friend! You remember me! Imagine that!"

"It is not so difficult to imagine," said Marcie. "No doubt he's never forgotten you."

Jack and the dog gave themselves over to a happy moment of tumbling in the snow. Jack grabbed the sheepdog by the scruff of his great neck and shook him lovingly, all the while crooning soft words. The faithful dog rewarded him with several more licks.

Miss Deirdre came up behind them then, stepping gingerly over the snowy footbridge. "Good heavens!" cried she, seeing Jack rolling in the snow with the dog. "Our highwayman is being attacked!"

"Nonsense," said Marcie. "He is merely greeting an old friend. Say hello to Bart, Miss Deirdre."

"Bart? Do not say that someone has actually given the beastie a name!"

Jack laughed, playfully pushing the dog away from him. He got to his feet, brushing the snow from his clothes. "Bart be no beastie, Miss Deirdre. He was once a pup I helped deliver myself, years past. I named him, too," he added proudly.

Miss Deirdre, backing away from the dog, managed to look long enough at Jack to see his eyes shining with bright memories.

Marcie saw the woman's features soften.

"You named him?" Miss Deirdre asked.

"That I did," replied Jack proudly. "Here, come give him a scratch behind his ears. Bart likes nothing better than to have his ears scratched."

Somewhat awkwardly, Jack reached for Miss Deirdre's finely gloved hand. The woman drew in a surprised gasp at Jack's touch—but she didn't pull away. Very gently, Jack drew her hand toward the sheepdog, who now sat complacently on its haunches at Jack's feet.

"That's it," whispered Jack. "Just a gentle scratch, that be all Bart needs. Ah, you've got him interested now. See how he bends his head your way?"

Miss Deirdre actually smiled. "Oh!" she said. "I—I had never thought to . . . to scratch a dog before, but I rather like it."

Jack beamed. "Makes you feel good inside, eh?"

Miss Deirdre fluttered her long lashes. "Indeed," she murmured, having eyes only for Jack.

Marcie shook her head, leaving the two to their silly conversation. She was more interested in reaching the vicarage and meeting the family who dwelled within.

With Prinny once again settled atop her shoulder, she hastened up the path, leaving the others in her wake. The chance to acquaint herself with a large and loving family drew her on. Though Marcie had been happy living alone with her father in Cornwall, she'd not been able to help wondering how different her life might have been had her father kept her in London where she would have been able to share secrets with her cousin, Meredith, and with Mirabella, who visited from far off lands now and then. Too, being an only child left Marcie ever longing for a large and extended family. Oh, to have lived within a home that was filled with constant commotion and much to-do! Marcie would have liked that; very much so, in fact. And someday, the good Lord willing, Marcie would meet the man of her dreams, and together they would create a parcel of children who would tug at her skirts and fill their home with the sounds of laughter and chaos.

To her delight, a number of children, screaming with glee, came sliding down a small hill. Marcie raced to greet them, heralding them all over a "finish line" that was naught but a line of ground holly laid down with loving care.

"A winner!" Marcie yelled as they came skimming across the holly on strips of leather.

Three small bodies tumbled happily into the snow.

Marcie laughed with the children. "Famous!" she cried.

The smallest of the children glanced up at Marcie and Prinny.

"An owl!" cooed the girl, delighted. "I've never been this close to an owl before."

"No? Then do come closer," replied Marcie. "Prinny is a very friendly owl."

The girl did as Marcie suggested and even reached up with one mittened hand to gently pat the owl on its head. She giggled as Prinny's eyes widened. "Is it true what the vicar tells me," she asked, "that all birds sing loudly and choose their mate on the morning of Saint Valentine's Day?"

Marcie had heard that same saying when she'd been very young, and she, too, had been caught up in the wonder and magic of what one special day might be able to create in the hearts of all God's creatures.

"I think," Marcie replied softly, "that it just may be so."

The girl inclined her head to one side, studying Marcie. "Are you one of Cupid's helpers? The vicar's wife told me today that Cupid and all of his helpers visit people on Saint Valentine's Day. And they bring love, and sometimes presents."

Marcie laughed. "I am not one of Cupid's helpers," she said. "But I've lots of gifts in my portmanteau—that is, if you like fossils."

"What kind of fossils?" the wide-eyed girl asked.

"Fossils from near the sea," said Marcie in a whispered voice. "Fossils straight from a smuggler's cave."

The girl gasped. "Really and truly?"

"Really and truly," said Marcie. "What is your name?"

"Frederica. But everyone calls me Freddie."

"Hello, Freddie. My name is Marcie. Pleased I am to make your acquaintance."

"Would you like to slide down the hill with my friends and me?" asked Freddie shyly.

Marcie didn't need to think twice. "Most definitely," she said. "I would be honored."

And so it was that Marcie, having set Prinny atop her portmanteau, helped pull the strips of leather back to the apex of the hill, waving as she went to Nan, Jack and Miss Deirdre, who were heading for the house. Cole Coachman, still dealing with his high-strung horses, was only now making his way over the footbridge.

Marcie grinned mischievously. If she figured correctly, she could make it to the hilltop and come winging down at just the precise moment Cole Coachman came through the gate of the vicarage. She felt a burning urge to give him a proper greeting to such a loving household. Surely happy children come to greet him would make the man smile!

So thinking, Marcie headed for the top of the hill.

* * *

Cole found himself cursing soundly as his nervous horses fidgeted yet again. Lord, but would they never reach the warm stall Jack had promised? Cole was close to losing his patience. He'd been led through everything short of a bramble patch. God only knew what manner of house Jack would guide them to. No doubt a shambles, thought Cole testily just as he managed to lead his cattle through a dense copse.

The sight of a welcoming and weather-worn vicarage, all brick and with three chimneys softly puffing smoke up into the snow-filled air, was not at all what he'd expected.

Cole straightened, thinking perhaps this day wasn't truly lost. He headed for the footbridge and the house past the low wall. It wasn't a fancy house, to be sure, but it appeared welcoming enough, lighted as it was behind the many frosted windows.

A young lad met him at the gate, with a warm welcome. "Jack asked me to take your horses to the stable, sir," said the youth, his cheeks bright from the cold. "Said I should rub them down good. Said I'd be rewarded with a shiny coin for my troubles."

Cole had no doubt but that Jack had also intended for Cole to be the one to produce the coin. No matter. Cole was just thankful to see that his horses would not be forced to endure further hardship in some drafty barn.

He handed the lad coin enough to make the boy's eyes wide as saucers, then watched as the youngster skillfully took charge of the horses. Assured they would be properly handled, Cole turned his gaze to the vicarage. Hearing the distant yip of a dog, he headed inside the stone wall.

Ah, finally, a peaceful haven at last, he thought . . . until he took several steps on the well-worn path. That was when all hell broke loose.

Suddenly, a seeming army of youngsters popped up from behind the hedge, pelting him with snowballs. Cole quickly moved to dodge the spheres of snow. Unfortunately, he stepped directly into the path of something moving fast down from the hilltop.

"Coming through!" called a very familiar, female voice.

Cole glanced up just in time to see Marcie plowing down upon him. "Oh, for the love of—"

Cole didn't have time to finish his exclamation. Instinctively, he dived out of harm's way, landing firmly in a snowbank just as Marcie veered sharply to the right and she and her new-found friends tumbled—laughing all the while—into the snow beside him. For the second time since he'd met her, Miss Marcelon Victoria Darlington had succeeded in seeing him covered from nose to toes in snow.

Cole came up sputtering, fully prepared to mutter a string of oaths. The number of children surrounding him, their loud voices, woefully reminded him of his numerous, demanding nieces. Too many times in his past he had been sorely tested by the spoilt offspring of his brothers.

But something was different about this group of snowball-throwing children. And the sight of his Mischievous Miss Marcie, giggling with heartfelt abandon and hugging a tiny girl lovingly to her chest, made his heart do a queer flip-flop.

Cole found himself stunned into speechlessness by the bright sparkle of happiness lighting Marcie's green eyes. And the children surrounding her, though loud and unreined, seemed not to gaze at Cole expectantly, but rather with happy faces that anticipated nothing more from him than his shared merriment in their winter play.

Miss Marcie wiped tears of laughter from her lovely face. "We did not cause you injury, did we?" she asked, most concerned. "I intended only to whisk near you and wish you a happy Saint Valentine's Day!"

Cole felt a perfect fool for thinking the children, or even Marcie, had harbored plots of deceit. He stood, brushing the snow from his greatcoat as he did so. "I am quite fine," he said. "And you?"

"Breathless," she said, truthfully. "I'd quite forgotten what fun it is to slide down a hill!"

Lord, but she was pretty; bonnet woefully askew, hair all tousled, cheeks pink, and her smile wide. Cole decided she'd never looked lovelier. He hastily minded his manners, offering her a hand out of the snow. The smallness of her gloved hand in his reminded him of the moment he'd tumbled down a road bank with her, when Miss Deirdre's coachman had nearly crashed into his coach. He found he liked the memory. If Marcie noticed that he'd allowed his grasp to linger overly long, she made no show of it.

"Allow me to introduce Mistress Frederica—known as Freddie—and her playmates, Masters Neville and Theodore," said Marcie, nodding to the youngsters.

Cole shook his thoughts away from the feel of Marcie's hand in his. He swept his hat from his head, giving a jaunty and exaggerated bow to the young miss and her friends.

Little Freddie giggled. Masters Neville and Theodore, Neville nervously blinking, and Theodore popping his mittened thumb out of his mouth, promptly executed like bows.

Marcie nodded toward the trio of snowball-throwing boys standing near. "And we must not forget Master Tom, Master John, and Master Richard," she said, adding, "but I haven't a clue who is who for Freddie had time enough only to rattle off their names as we flew down the hill."

Cole tipped a grin their way as the boys stepped forward, reciting their names and ages. As it turned out, Marcie had introduced them in order of age.

Thomas, the eldest, had watched with an appreciative eye as Cole led the horses inside the stone wall. Thomas said as much, and soon Cole and the young boy were talking horseflesh. Cole felt his heart warm even more when little Freddie gave a tug to his sleeve, asking if she might be able to give a pet to his team.

Cole found himself being led by the hand to the stable, where the boys and little Freddie cooed over his cattle and Miss Marcie, smiling fondly over the group, stood at his side, Prinny perched on her shoulder. They stayed at the stable for better than an hour, the children helping to rub down the fine beasts, check their hooves, and seeing to their welfare.

Cole couldn't ever remember enjoying the presence of children as much as he did at that moment. How odd. Children, until now, had always presented problems, not comfort—and certainly not joy—to Cole.

But with Marcie gently encouraging the children to be nothing more than, well, children, the time seemed to fly past on wings. There was much giggling and sharing of stories as the boys and little Freddie fawned over the cattle.

Too soon for Cole, Jack came to retrieve the lot of them and lead them into the vicarage. Cole at first thought the magical moments shared in the stable would be lost to him, but he was surprisingly mistaken. There proved to be more merriment within the vicarage.

Vicar Clarke, a rotund fellow with thinning hair and a heart as wide as an ocean, could not have given a warmer welcome. He and his wife, a tiny sparrow of a woman who had the patience of a saint, were the perfect host and host-ess. As for their brood of lively orphans, they proved to be just as open and giving and sweetly curious as they had been in the stables.

Since the snow continued to fall in great, huge flakes, the vicar and his wife insisted that Cole and his passengers remain for a few hours at the vicarage, or at least until the tail end of the storm waned. They were generous enough to offer them a meal and some entertainment, and Prinny a perch on an ancient hat rack in the hall.

Following an ample—and decidedly lively—luncheon, the guests were led to a parlour where Marcie helped young Freddie play a tune upon an old and untuned pianoforte. The notes proved flat and erroneous, but Marcie, turning the pages of the music sheets, added both laughter and her own pretty singing voice to help make the unsteady tune a success.

Cole would have liked to prop up his feet and chase away the day within the warm vicarage. It had been many hours since he'd last slept, but he knew he must finish his run, and said as much.

Jack, surprisingly enough to Cole, assured him that enough hands would be sent for to help dig the Mail coach from its snowy trap. Both Jack and Vicar Clarke made certain the three oldest lads were sent to a neighboring farm for assistance.

Meanwhile, Miss Deirdre, complaining of cold toes, was led to an upstairs bed chamber by the vicar's wife to find some warmth and comfort. Nan, following behind, offered to help thaw the lady's clothes by the hearth, and Jack, with Bart at his heels, took to combing the halls of the vicarage in search of memories from his youth, while Vicar Clarke and the three boys made haste to find help in freeing Cole's coach.

Cole blinked in astonishment as nearly everyone departed the cosy room—everyone, that was, but young Freddie, the nervous Neville, the thumb-sucking Theodore, and, of course, Miss Marcie.

It seemed to Cole that Marcie was at a loss as to what to do now that her thief and their hosts had scurried away. She leafed through the music sheets, making a motion to put them into some order. She miserably abandoned the act when Freddie piped up to say that the music sheets were in no particular order but were thrown haphazardly onto the bench whenever she was finished practicing her chords.

"I like my sheets in a mess," Freddie said with childlike candor. "No need to straighten them, Miss Marcie. Half the fun is trying to find a certain sheet."

Little Freddie immediately made chaos of any order Marcie had tried to create. "There," she announced. "Now I shall have to spend several minutes searching for the proper sheet. I do declare that is what I like best! Making sense of nonsense is what Vicar Clarke says I do best of all."

Cole watched as Marcie beamed. "Why, Freddie," said Miss Marcie, "I do believe we are cut of the same cloth, for I too would make a game out of practicing. I once had a horrid schoolmistress who had no patience whatsoever for my constant shifting of the sheet music!"

Marcie laughed, and Cole felt his heart warm as she reached down to squeeze Freddie's hand. The sound of Marcie's laughter was like a chorus of wondrous bells in his brain, and the sight of her as she smiled lovingly at Freddie nigh took Cole's breath away.

How was it that Marcie had such power over his senses? One minute she could vex him mightily, and the next minute, with just a turn of her head or a soft smile, she could make his insides melt. Egad, but only a fool in love could

be forced through the gamut of emotions! Cole felt his heart
give a queer jerk at the thought. *Only a fool in love . . .*

Could it be?

No. Impossible!

Cole dragged his thoughts back to the present—just in
time to see Marcie's lovely green eyes catch the light of the
candles. He felt himself verily drowning in those sparkling
green depths.

In love. Ah, yes, it was indeed possible. Trouble was,
Marcie thought him to be Cole Coachman and not the Marquis of Sherringham.

Little Freddie suddenly leapt up from her bench and
raced to the window. She pressed her nose to the cold, iced
glass, and cooed with pleasure as she watched the snow
fall down to the ground outside.

"Can we not walk in the snow, Miss Marcie? Please? I
do so like to walk while the snow is falling! Oh, say that
we may. Please do!"

Cole thought Marcie must surely have had enough of the
cold day and was surprised when she followed the girl to the
window, leading both Neville and Theodore alongside her.

"A walk in the snow, hm?" she said softly, kneeling down
beside the girl and the boys.

"Oh, yes," said young Freddie. "I would like that very
much!"

The boys added enthusiastic cries, and soon Miss Marcie
was heading for her wrap.

Cole found himself sitting upright. He suddenly did not
want to be left out of anything Marcie and the children
enjoyed, though God knew he'd had enough of the snow
and the cold. He was out of his chair before he knew what
he was about. He reached for Marcie's hand.

"Pray, allow me to join you," he found himself saying.

Miss Marcie hesitated. "Truly, you need not go back out into the cold. I shall walk with the children down to the bridge and back, just far enough for them to enjoy the snowfall, but you needn't feel you must join us. I know how arduous your journey has been and—"

"No more arduous than yours," Cole interrupted.

"Yes," Marcie agreed, "but I enjoyed the comfort of the inside coach while you were forced to endure the cold and blowing winds."

"It is what all good coachmen must endure."

"And you are that," she said softly, catching Cole unawares with the whispery gentleness of her melodic voice. "You are indeed a fine coachman, Cole."

Cole found himself quite tongue-tied by her heartfelt compliment. "Why, I am . . . uh . . . most pleased by your kind words," he said, uncharacteristically tripping over the words.

His lordship felt a rush of remorse wash over him. This lovely miss would doubtless feel deceived—and rightly so—if ever she should learn he wasn't an ordinary coachman but rather the Marquis of Sherringham. Cole knew very well she would have acted differently with him had she known of his title.

Though he very much wished to share with her the truth of his identity, he knew he could not. Not yet, anyway. To do so would mean having to witness the brightness in her beautiful eyes dim, and what a pity that would be, for it was the twinkle in her eyes that he liked best about her.

In all honesty, Cole had to admit that he rather liked playing the part of a coachman, for it was that very guise that allowed him to cast off all his cares and woes and be himself. Had Marcie known of his title, she would not have been so candid with him, he knew. Indeed, she most likely would never have flagged him down near the snowy mews of her boarding school and Cole would not have had the pleasure of being in her company. What a perfect shame that would have been!

No, Cole decided. He would not mar this moment with the truth of his identity.

Cole guided her hand to the crook of his right elbow. "Shall we?" he said, his heart suddenly feeling light as air.

Miss Marcie smiled.

Together, they led the children outside into the snow.

Cole could not remember ever enjoying himself as much as he did during their leisurely stroll.

Huge snowflakes twirled through the air. In the distance could be heard the tinkling of bells and the nickering of horses. The children bounded ahead, little Freddie twirling with abandon as she went and then dropping down into the snow to create angel wings with her arms. Masters Neville and Theodore engaged in yet another snowball fight, and their antics urged Cole and Marcie into a run as they playfully dodged the spheres of snow.

Little Freddie declared a race to the bridge, jumping up out of the snow to scurry down the path. Both Theodore and Neville chased after her, throwing snowballs as they ran. By the time they reached the footbridge, all of them—Cole included—were laughing with delight.

The children skidded down the bank, picking their way over the ice-encrusted rocks, the boys searching for an imaginary footpad beneath the bridge, and little Freddie announcing that she was positive one of Cupid's whimsical helpers might be found there as well.

A breathless Marcie leaned back against the weatherworn rail and tipped her face up to Cole. With an impish grin, she said, "You are laughing, My Lord Monarch. Do you know I have been racking my brain all morning, trying to devise a plan to see you do just that?"

Cole, a bit breathless himself, planted his forearms on the rail beside her. As he leaned forward, his face was close to hers. "I am not such a curmudgeon, am I?" he asked. "Surely you must have heard me laugh before this moment."

Marcie shook her head, molten curls bobbing with the motion. "Not like this," she said truthfully.

"So I have been a starchy bore, is that what you are saying?"

"A bore? Never! Starchy? Perhaps just a little," she playfully teased. "But I do understand that a fine coachman such as yourself is first and foremost concerned with his coach and his cattle."

Her smile widened, causing her lively eyes to shine like diamonds capturing both moon and starlight. Cole felt completely spellbound. Lord, she was pretty. And sweet. And honest to a fault. What a deceitful being he was not to tell her his true identity.

His conscience got the better of him.

"Please, if you will, I've something I've been meaning to tell you."

She looked up at him with clear green eyes.

"Yes?" she asked.

Cole felt his throat constrict.

Devil take it, but he'd never been tongue-tied with a woman as he was now. He knew he should just blurt out the truth. Be done with it.

"I . . . uh . . . I just wanted to say that I—I have enjoyed watching you with the vicar's charges," he suddenly heard himself say.

Oh, what a coward he was! Why the deuce couldn't he

just say it, admit he was not a mere coachman but a marquis with great wealth and a family name that stretched far into the exalted past of England?

But he knew why. The truth would only erect a thick wall between them. Young runaways from decrepit boarding schools did not dash through the snow with titled gentlemen. Cole held firm in his decision not to bring his true identity to light.

"You might be a runaway schoolgirl, Miss Marcie, but you certainly have a heart of gold where children are concerned," he said instead, and meant every word he uttered.

Marcie blushed prettily. "I've a soft spot in my soul for large families, Cole," she said. "I am an only child, you know. I can't tell you how often I've wished that I grew up in a busy, hectic household."

Cole heaved a mental sigh of relief, suddenly glad he hadn't ruined the magical moment. Said he, "Then no doubt you would open your arms to a family such as mine."

"Oh? You've a large family?"

"Too large, I sometimes believe. I've so many spoilt nieces that I find myself wondering which way to turn. They are constantly demanding this and that of me. And their mothers, widowed as they are, seem to think I've nothing better to do than see to everyone's comfort and entertainment. I am not complaining," he added. "Only stating what is true. But I do believe that now I shall view my many nieces in a kinder light."

"And why is that?"

Cole nodded toward Masters Neville and Theodore, and little Freddie. "Because of them," he said softly. "And because of you."

Miss Marcie caught her breath. "But all we've done is walk in the snow. Surely, that is not so unusual."

Ah, if only she knew! The Marquis of Sherringham would never have thought to stroll in the snow; had he any free time—which he rarely, if ever, did—he would not think to fritter it away with anything so ridiculous as an aimless walk, instead choosing to attend to his numerous duties.

But his lordship, in the guise of Cole Coachman, could easily forget about the many pressing matters left behind in Town. Cole Coachman knew a heady freedom that the marquis, sadly enough, might never know. Cole as coachman could find beauty in a falling snowflake, could find joy in a child's laughter . . . and could find both wondrous peace and promising passion in the eyes of one very mischievous miss.

Cole drew his face closer to Marcie's. "Forgive me," he whispered, voice husky.

"Forgive you for what, Cole?"

"For this," he said.

And then he kissed her. With all his heart and soul, he kissed her.

Eleven

Marcie watched, mesmerized, as Cole lowered his lips toward hers. He paused momentarily, allowing her the chance to push him away if she so desired. But Marcie, all atremble inside, did not desire to do so. She very much wanted him to kiss her.

Marcie's lips parted ever so slightly as she drew in a quick breath, and then, quite suddenly, she felt the heat of his mouth whispering across her own. Sweetly, gently, he claimed her with a searing brand that left her knees feeling deliciously weak and her heart soaring to great heights. *This,* she thought dreamily, *is how every Saint Valentine's Day should be. With this handsome man pressing his lips to her mouth, with children frolicking near, and the possibility of love lingering all about. . . .*

He lifted one hand, sliding it slowly against her throat to curl his fingers at the base of her neck while his other hand slipped around her waist to nestle at the small of her back. Breathing in the scent of spice and cedar that emanated from his greatcoat, Marcie melted against his hard-muscled frame. How warm and wonderful he felt. And how oddly safe she felt in his embrace.

Though she was inexperienced, she instinctively knew how to respond to him as he playfully teased the corners of her mouth. *Oh my!* she thought, even as she gave herself over to the moment and returned his fervent embrace, *surely a well-bred young lady would not allow a man such liberties.*

But she wasn't a well-bred young lady, Marcie reminded herself; she'd only been trying to be one since journeying to Mistress Cheltenham's horrid school. In truth, she was naught but the wild, mischievous daughter of a wealthy Cit who had never, ever given himself over to the dictates of a too-strict society. And that, coupled with the fact that she was heading to her godmama's home only to be introduced to some stuffy swell, who might or might not become her intended, made Marcie enjoy Cole Coachman's brazen kiss all the more. She gave herself over to the wondrous sensations coursing through her, opening to Cole like a flower to the sun.

Marcie was surprised at how easily their bodies melded together. Surely this kiss was meant to be, thought Marcie, nearly mad with pleasure and delight. How silly she'd been to believe Cole had designs on the worldly Miss Deirdre. If that were so, he wouldn't be kissing her; indeed, he never would have bothered to join her for a stroll in the snow but would have lingered in the parlour to await the reappearance of the golden-haired beauty.

Marcie sighed, drinking in the man's sweet kiss, believing, finally, that he wasn't the moody cock o' the road she'd previously thought him to be. Instead, he had proved to be gentle, and caring, and far too appealing.

Marcie wished the kiss could go on and on.

Interference, though, came in the form of three young bodies popping up from beneath the bridge.

"Ooooh," crooned little Freddie. "I never seen anyone kiss like that! Do you think they are in love?"

"If that not be love," said Master Neville, "then it be something we ought not be seeing."

Master Theodore sucked loudly on the mittened thumb of his right hand, grinning all the while.

Marcie and Cole abruptly parted, both of them turning to peer down at Freddie, Neville, and Theodore who now stood on the icy rocks of the streambed, their elbows propped up on the base of the bridge, their eyes near popping out of their heads.

Little Freddie, chin cupped in her mittened hands, sighed with romantic drama. "Oh, do kiss Miss Marcie some more, Cole Coachman. Please do!"

Masters Neville and Theodore continued to grin like cats who'd found a saucer full of cream.

Marcie blushed.

Cole Coachman swore beneath his breath. "Have you nothing better to do than spy on your elders?" he demanded, placing a respectable distance between himself and Marcie.

"Oh, drat," muttered Freddie. "He *isn't* going to kiss her again!"

The little girl frowned, but a moment later she'd quite forgotten her disappointment when a sled pulled by a plow horse came winging through the snow up the lane toward the vicarage.

"Visitors!" exclaimed little Freddie.

Freddie and the boys scrambled up the stream-bank, then raced to meet the sled. Marcie, too, turned to watch the sleigh wind its way toward the vicarage.

Help in freeing Cole's coach had arrived.

Marcie's heart fell; she would soon be leaving the vicarage, and the children, and the stolen moments she and Cole had shared.

She wasn't at all pleased.

* * *

Cole bit back a sharp expletive at the sight of the sled. He should have been pleased at how quickly the vicar and his charges had whipped up a ready team of hands and muscle to help pull his Mail coach free of the snowdrift. But he wasn't.

To free his coach meant he must press on toward the inn at Burford—an inn that stood too near. At the inn, he knew, his Mistress Mischief would take her leave of him. And he, alas, would face the remainder of Saint Valentine's Day without her.

"It appears as though we shall reach Burford before the end of the day," he said.

Miss Marcie nodded. "Yes," she agreed, voice quiet. She did not turn to look at him.

"That is still your wish, is it not? To be taken to the inn at Burford?" He hoped—no, he prayed—she would reply in the negative.

"Of—of course," she murmured, causing Cole's heart to fall. "Burford does indeed remain my point of destination."

Cole swallowed his disappointment past the sudden and unexpected lump in his throat. "And what will you do there, My Mistress Mischief?" he asked, unable to stop himself from voicing the question.

She finally turned, tipping her face up to his. Her green eyes shimmered—though whether the spark was due to his term of endearment, or due to the fact she would soon be at the inn, Cole could not decipher.

"I shall commence to try and enjoy the holiday," she answered. "But what of you, My Lord Monarch? What roads will you take once we reach Burford?"

Oh, God, but he couldn't think straight, not when she was looking so pretty and so . . . lost. Was that it? Lost? No, she couldn't be feeling lost, not when she was all but assured of reaching her desired destination. Surely Cole was imagining things.

"I shall guide my coach ever northward, routing the last few parcels and Valentine's gifts a few close acquaintances entrusted me to deliver."

"And when might you take a moment to enjoy the specialness of Saint Valentine's Day, Cole?"

When indeed? he thought.

"Soon," he answered. *Probably never,* he thought, *not if he could not have Marcie near him.*

Cole had taken on the run only to avoid the parties, the many demands of his station, and the ceaseless chatter of his nieces and sisters-in-law. Saint Valentine's Day had ever been a tiresome holiday to endure in the past. It always seemed that whatever party he attended in the days before Saint Valentine's Day, the ladies there would glance at him with expectation, no doubt in the hope that he would prove to be their secret suitor. There was ever someone wanting something of him, demanding this and that of him, and of course, he had yet to find, until now, that one special other with which to share the day intended for lovers. And so, Cole had struck out on the roads in the guise of Cole Coachman with only one thought in mind: Freedom.

Cole marveled at the fact that he'd found such freedom in the form of a mischievous miss from some snowy mews. This girl, with curls framing her pixie face, and her mobile mouth forming the sweetest of smiles, had shown him what he'd been missing these many years past since he'd ascended to the title. He'd not truly been living but rather going through the motions of life, more concerned with ledgers and appearances, never bothering to admire the beauty of a snowfall, to be swept away by a child's laugh, or to look

beneath the surface of a bedraggled highwayman. Marcie
had taught Cole to do all those things.

Cole suddenly wished their kiss hadn't been interrupted,
for he very much would have liked to end it with a few
heartfelt words. He wanted to tell Marcie he wished to
spend more time with her, that he wished to court her. He
wanted to tell her so many things.

But he couldn't. She was but a runaway school miss,
enjoying her first foray into a wide world. She obviously
had great plans to put into motion once she reached the inn
at Burford. Ah, to be a part of those plans. . . .

Cole mentally frowned. He had no place in her mischievous, hectic, wonderfully thrilling life. He was a titled gentleman, quite stuffy and too much wrapped up in the many
coils his sisters-in-law and nieces pulled him into.

Also, there was the matter of a certain heiress whom he
was destined to become acquainted with at the home of
Penelope Barrington. His sisters-in-law, surprisingly enough,
were in unanimous agreement that Cole should meet this heiress and eventually marry her. The fact that they were suddenly
pushing him toward marriage was quite puzzling to Cole; in
the event he didn't marry, their children would each stand to
inherit staggering sums. But suddenly, his sisters-in-law were
preoccupied with the fact that Cole had not taken a fancy to
the pretty ladies of the ton. That they'd come to agree on a
wealthy Cit's daughter as his chosen intended was more than
a little suspect.

What possible motive had they for doing such a thing?
He knew not. Unless, of course, his sisters-in-law were truly
concerned with his happiness. Could it be possible their
matchmaking attempt was a generous and purely unselfish
act? The more Cole thought about it, the more he knew it
to be true.

Cole knew now he must at least make an appearance at Penelope's party. Though he vowed to be rid of the Cit heiress as soon as possible—since all the heiresses he'd met thus far had been unutterably hen-witted and spoilt and no one would be able to hold a candle to Marcie—he would at least show his sisters-in-law his respect by attending Penelope's Saint Valentine's Day ball.

With all this in mind, Cole reluctantly owned up to the fact that a future with his Mistress Mischief was not to be. She was enjoying her first taste of freedom. No doubt she would be fast and far away by the time he made his required appearance at Penelope's estate.

Cole sighed.

"I suppose I should lead you back inside," he said. "You'll want to warm yourself by the hearth before we again begin our journey. And I must help the others free my coach."

"Yes," she said.

Was that sadness he perceived in those bewitching eyes of hers? Surely it couldn't be. What had she to be forlorn about? She was almost to Burford, her grand escape from boarding school nearly a success. No doubt she was just tired. They'd traveled many miles in a very short time. Yes, she was tired. That was all.

Cole tucked her hand in the crook of his arm and led her back up the path to the vicarage. It was a walk he wished would have no end.

But end it did, and far too soon for Cole. They'd no sooner stepped inside the entrance than little Freddie, having come inside with the others, came racing down the hall, crying with delight and throwing herself into Marcie's arms. Marcie barely had time enough to shed her cloak—with Cole's assistance—than the girl was pulling Marcie along, begging her to share some of the fossils in her portmanteau.

Marcie laughed, and the light trill of her laughter near took Cole's breath away. Ah, but she was a delight to see, and to hear . . . and to kiss.

Cole stepped forward, ever concerned about Marcie's welfare. He got down on bent knees before little Freddie.

With a soft voice meant only for the child's ears, he said, "I hope you will not overly tire Miss Marcie. I know you are fond of her, and she of you, but she is tired from her journey. I am worried about her. May I rely upon you to see that she rests while I and the others head out into the cold to free my coach? Will you do this for me, Freddie?"

That he'd gotten down on bent knees to speak to this tiny slip of a girl astonished Cole, and the fact that he was speaking to her so frankly was quite beyond his own belief. He had never, ever spoken to any of his nieces with such candor, and yet he felt very much at ease speaking thus to this little orphan. It was the magic of one Marcelon Victoria Darlington, to be sure, that made his hard heart thaw and open up to this smiling, beautiful girl.

Freddie beamed with delight. She grasped his face in her chubby little hands, drew her face close to his right ear, and whispered, "Oooh, I just knew you loved her. I knew it by the way you kissed her down at the bridge. Cupid has made you fall in love with Miss Marcie!"

Cole felt himself blush for the first time in his entire life. "Ahem," he muttered, quite taken by surprise. "Well now, that shall be our own secret, shall it not?"

"Oh, yes," she whispered. "Cross my heart!"

Freddie stepped back, making a tiny cross over the place where her heart beat, giving Cole a wink as she did so.

Cole chucked her under the chin. His entire being was engulfed with a warm sensation as he got to his feet. He watched as Freddie commenced to drag Marcie down the hall, toward the portmanteau and the promised fossils. A part of him wished to join them while his saner half knew that he must cut all ties with Marcie, and the sooner the better. He had no place in her carefree world.

He felt a hand on his shoulder. Turning, he found Miss Deirdre, looking resplendent in a fresh gown, her hair combed to a high sheen and pulled back into a comely cascade, leaning against him.

"You must help me, Cole Coachman," she said in a fast whisper. "I do believe I am in quite a fix!"

"Whatever is the matter?" asked Cole.

"I cannot possibly share my tale with you here. Come, we must find someplace private. The library will suffice."

And with that, Cole found himself bodily dragged into the library by the passionate Miss Deirdre.

Marcie, tripping down the hall behind little Freddie, glanced over her shoulder just in time to see Miss Deirdre, who looked too gorgeous for words, pressing her comely shape against Cole's side. The woman whispered something into the man's ear, and then, quite brazenly, thought Marcie, led him into a room just off the hall. The latch of the door fell firmly into place behind them.

Marcie's heart fell to the pit of her stomach with the sound. So, Cole had just been toying with her when he'd kissed her. What a fool she'd been to allow him such liberties! Oh, but surely he must have inwardly laughed at her unskilled and awkward attempt at returning his kiss!

Marcie's face burned with shame.

What a stupid, idiotic chit she'd been. The Cole Coachmans of the world would never find someone as green as her intriguing. They would toy with her, certainly, but they would never take her seriously . . . not when the likes of the worldly Miss Deirdre offered all a man could desire.

As Marcie and Freddie reached her portmanteau and began sorting through the fossils, searching for some that caught Freddie's fancy, Marcie felt the sting of bitter tears burn her eyes.

"Miss Marcie?" Little Freddie suddenly forgot the fossils. "You are crying. Why? Have I made you angry? Do you not wish to share your fossils with me?"

Marcie dashed the wetness from her eyes. "Oh, no, sweetheart, that is not it. Not at all."

"Then why are you crying?"

"I—I am just tired, I think. I'm so very tired." And cold, she thought. Her heart had frozen at the sight of Cole so easily trailing after the comely Miss Deirdre.

"Come," said little Freddie softly. "I know a very special place where you can rest."

Marcie, her thoughts with Cole and Miss Deirdre, blindly followed little Freddie along a maze of hallways and then up a steep set of back stairs that wound round and round. She felt as though she were climbing up into a dark, solitary place. Marcie didn't care. She only wanted to get far away from the place where Cole and Miss Deirdre were no doubt locked in each other's embrace.

Cole stumbled into an unlit room.

"Such a web I've made for myself!" Miss Deirdre wailed once she latched the door behind him. "You must help me, Cole!"

"Oh, bother," muttered Cole, having slammed his left knee into something hard and ungiving. "Why the devil did you have to lead us into the darkest room of this monstrous place? Light a light, I beg you!"

Miss Deirdre clicked her tongue in exasperation, moving away from him even as she did so. Cole heard the swish of heavy drapes. He winced as daylight streamed inside the frosted windows.

"Much better," he muttered, looking down to see the object he'd smashed into was a dusty, wing-backed chair.

Miss Deirdre whirled away from the windows, facing him with all the calm of a coming hurricane.

"I have quite fallen in love with the wrong man!" she cried.

Cole blinked. Could she mean him? Lord, but he hoped not.

Feeling guilty for having been so attentive to her during his run, he said: "There is something you should know about me, Miss Deirdre—"

"Please," she interrupted hastily, "but I haven't the where-withal to deal with your confessions of undying love. I tell you, man, I am in a fix! *I am quite head over heels in love with your highwayman!*"

Stunned, Cole could do nothing more than gape at her. "Wh—what did you say?" he asked, not able to believe the words she'd just uttered.

"I know, I know," Miss Deirdre said, pacing the floor. "You thought me to be quite enamored of you . . . and I *was,* to a point. But then I met Jack."

"Jack?"

"Yes. Jack. Do keep your voice down! I shouldn't want word of this getting around. Not, that is, until I wish it to be known. Oh, Cole, whatever shall I *do?*"

Cole plunked himself down into the wing-backed chair,

getting a nose full of dust for his troubles. He began to laugh.

"I find nothing amusing in all of this!" Miss Deirdre cried. "How dare you laugh at me! I'll have you know I have been mistress to the Regent himself! Indeed Prinny is expecting me to grace his bed again very soon! But the fact is, I find him quite dull—God save my neck for admitting this—in comparison to our wonderfully unkempt but manly highwayman!"

Laughing all the more, Cole threw back his head.

Miss Deirdre stamped one foot on the floor. "Oh!" she exclaimed. "What would a lowly coachman know of such things! I don't know why I ever bothered to let you in on my secret."

Cole sobered somewhat. "Perhaps," he said, "it is because I am not a lowly coachman but rather the Marquis of Sherringham. Allow me to introduce myself. I am Cole Charles Edward Sherringham, known to the ton as Sherry . . . and known along the road as simply Cole Coachman."

"Say it isn't so!" exclaimed Miss Deirdre.

"Ah, but it is," he said. "I am both lord and liar. A bore in Town and a fool on the road." He lifted one eyebrow toward her. "I, too, am in a fix, Miss Deirdre."

"You? How so? Obviously, you've coin and prestige enough to dig yourself out of any coil."

"Not by far, for, you see, this coil has to do with a woman . . . and my heart."

"Ah," whispered Miss Deirdre, enlightened. "You mean Marcie."

"Yes. Marcie."

"You have taken a fancy to her?"

"It goes deeper than that, I am afraid."

"You are in love with her."

"I wouldn't know, exactly. I have never been in love with a woman before."

"I find that difficult to believe. I have heard of you, Sherry . . . er, Cole . . . er, my lord—"

"Let us keep things simple, shall we? Call me Cole and be done with it."

She nodded. "You are considered quite a catch among the ladies of the ton, Cole. Surely, you have fallen in love a time or two."

" 'Twas only lust I'd fallen into in the past, and then had to claw my way out of it. But with Marcie, everything is different. All things are new and fresh and exciting, and— damn! but I cannot articulate all she makes me feel."

"I think you just have."

Cole blew out an exasperated sigh. "It matters not a whit," he said. "The miss has her sights set on reaching the inn at Burford, at which point she fully intends to embark on a life of unfettered freedom. No doubt she would balk at becoming my wife and forced to endure the insufferable hectic social whirl I took to the roads to escape."

"Yes," sighed Miss Deirdre, staring off into a dark corner of the room. "My Jack seems to like his freedom as well."

The two of them fell silent, stewing in their own miserable thoughts. Miss Deirdre commenced pacing back and forth in front of the windows, while Cole stared at his booted toes as though the answer to his predicament might suddenly appear there.

"I have it!" exclaimed Miss Deirdre suddenly.

"Have what?" Cole demanded, startled by her loud exclamation.

"A plan, of course!"

"Of course. Do tell," he said. "I am all ears." Fact was, he hadn't any plans of his own short of tearing through the

vicarage in search of Marcie and then throwing himself—
and his undying love—at her pretty feet. Not a very imagi-
native plot, to be sure. And one, certainly, that would leave
him to lick his wounds in private once his mischievous miss
learned of his title and that he wasn't a true monarch of
the road.

Miss Deirdre tapped one long-nailed finger against her
lovely chin. "All our troubles would be solved if only we
had a Cupid in our midst," she said thoughtfully. "The only
question remains, whom shall we choose to play Cupid?"

"I haven't a clue," said Cole, though thoughts of little
Freddie, who believed in Cupids and arrows of love, tripped
through his brain. But no. He'd not stoop to using a young
orphan to do his bidding.

"The answer is simple," said Miss Deirdre. "I shall be
your Cupid, and you, Cole, shall be mine!"

"What the devil are you proposing?"

"A very simple thing, actually. You need only become a
tick in Jack's ear. Sway him in my direction. That is all I
need; I assure you I can handle things from that point on.
As for your Marcie, I shall sing your praises to her. I'll
have her realizing that any day not spent with you would
be an utter bore. Oh! Do you not think it a wonderful idea?"

Cole had his reservations. "Jack and I haven't exactly
been bosom friends during this run," he said. And Marcie,
he knew, wasn't exactly enamored of the too-beautiful Miss
Deirdre.

Miss Deirdre waved away his worries. "Jack has a huge
heart. He'll warm to you soon enough, but you have to
make the first move."

"And Marcie?" he asked.

"She's a woman, isn't she? We speak the same language.

Do not fear. I shall have your bird-loving miss eating out of your hand in no time," Miss Deirdre assured him.

Trouble was, Cole didn't want Marcie "eating out of his hand" as Miss Deirdre put it. He wanted her to want him as much as he wanted her. He desired, begad, to meet her on equal footing. No subterfuge. No half-truths. Just the two of them, coming together because they could do no less. And he wanted, more than anything, to join her on the road to freedom and happiness, their hands clasped together and their hearts and their steps in tune with each other.

"I don't know," he muttered, wary. "Perhaps Nan should be my Cupid." Or even little Freddie, he thought.

"Dismiss that idea!" said Miss Deirdre, moving toward him to pull him up and out of the chair. "Nan would no doubt lose her train of thought should a bit of food be whisked beneath her nose! No, I am the person to play your Cupid. After all, I have caught the jaded eye of Prinny himself. I know exactly how to make your young Marcie turn her head your way, do not worry!"

But Cole did worry.

Twelve

Marcie, feet curled beneath her on the window seat Freddie had led her to, leaned her head back against the frame of the window and sighed heavily. Little Freddie had gone below in search of some tea for Marcie to drink, leaving Marcie alone in the cosy little alcove, where Freddie obviously spent much of her time.

Marcie smiled when she spied a ragged doll propped up against the opposite corner. She reached for the doll. Its porcelain face was chipped by wear and cracked with age, but the tiny dress it wore was clearly new and recently pressed. There was a snowy white blanket beneath it, and beneath that, Marcie could see a heart etched into the wood of the window seat.

Marcie cradled the doll in one arm, then leaned forward to better read the inscription carved into the center of the heart: *C.C. loves Miss M. 1793.*

Obviously, someone just as much in love as she was now had sat upon this very seat and painstakingly carved those letters. What bittersweet coincidence that her initials and Cole's matched to perfection.

Marcie let out a soft, ragged sigh. Tears moistened her eyes. She sat there alone, clutching Freddie's chipped and worn doll, and wishing, ever wishing, that things could turn out differently for herself and Cole Coachman.

* * *

Marcie, so caught up in her own miserable thoughts, scarcely noticed the sounds of little Freddie climbing the stairs, Jack in tow.

Freddie peeked through the archway leading to the secluded window seat high above the vicarage.

"She be crying!" Freddie gasped. "Oh, you must do something, Jack!"

"But what?" asked Jack, rubbing his whiskered jaw.

Little Freddie did not hesitate. "Why, tell her to march down the stairwell in search of your fine coachman. Marcie and Cole Coachman are ever so much in love with each other, I just know it!" Freddie suddenly slapped one tiny hand over her mouth. "Oh my," she muttered. "I swore I'd never tell! Oh, but I've made a mess of it, I have."

Jack screwed up his face in bewilderment. "A mess of what, child? Speak no more nonsense, please! You got me all in a tither, you have, what with your mutterings. Now what the blazes are you talking about?"

"Nothing," whispered, Freddie. "Everything. Oh, just go to her, Jack. Tell her to hurry downstairs and search for Cole Coachman. She won't listen to me as I am only a child."

Jack stared at her, hard. "A child wiser than the lot of us put together," he hazarded. "Stop your fussing. I be going, my little Freddie, have no fear. But I don't know that it will do any good. Miss Marcie be a headstrong lass. And Cole Coachman, he be as bendable as a bit of cold ore."

"But he has a soft heart," said Freddie.

"If you say so," muttered Jack. And before he knew it, he was stumbling up the last step and then into the tiny window alcove.

* * *

Marcie dashed away her tears at sight of Jack.

"Is Freddie all right?" she asked. "She didn't fall with the tea tray, did she? I told her I could get my own tea, but she was most adamant about bringing it up here to me."

"Freddie be fine," said Jack. "It is you I be worried about. Come now, what are you doing here, curled up like some sad angel?"

"Oh, Jack," whispered Marcie, all of her troubles pouring out of her. "It is Saint Valentine's Day, my most favorite of days, and yet . . . here I sit, being a perfect watering pot. My heart was broken by the passing of my father, and I told myself—no, I swore to myself—that I would never, ever allow my heart to be broken again. And yet, I have. It is breaking now, breaking as it never has. I love him, Jack. I love Cole Coachman . . . but he does not return my love."

Marcie fell against him, her tears running unchecked.

"Ah, sweetling," Jack murmured, catching her in an awkward embrace. "Jack here hates to see you suffer so. Please don't cry. My shabby coat cannot take the salty tears!"

"I—I am sorry," Marcie said. She hiccoughed. "I thought . . . I thought that Cole might return my feelings. But I realize now he could never love someone as green as me."

"You might be green, my lovely Marcie," said Jack passionately, "but I never met me a prettier or sweeter thing than you. Now you dry your eyes. Jack will set things right."

"No!" she said. Marcie knew very well that Cole did not hold the highwayman in high esteem. There was absolutely no way she would have Jack suffer Cole's moodiness on her account.

Marcie gently pulled away from him. "I thank you for

your kind offer Jack, but I cannot accept. You have done more than enough for me."

"Here now," he argued, "I managed to do nothing more than land you in hot water what with the dice throwing and all. And we both know your coachman was none too happy about that."

"But you led us here, to the vicarage. And," she added softly, smiling, "you taught me to how to dance."

"It was only a simple jig," he insisted.

"It was a lovely jig, and a very gentlemanly offer on your part. I thank you for it."

Jack blushed. He bowed his head, scratched his chin, and began to shift his weight from one foot to the other.

Marcie, realizing she'd embarrassed the man, decided to end the conversation. She placed Freddie's doll back on the window seat. That done, she turned to Jack, slipped one arm through the crook of his, and motioned toward the stairs.

"Shall we go below and join the others, Jack?"

He nodded, a twinkle lighting his eyes.

As Marcie led the way down the stairs, she told herself that she'd only been imagining things when she thought she'd perceived a plan forming in Jack's mind. Surely Jack would not be so bold as to speak to Cole on her behalf, would he? Lord, she hoped not.

A few minutes later, Marcie joined Nan and the vicar's wife in the huge kitchen downstairs. Nan was busy tasting the cake batter the vicar's wife was stirring. Both females greeted Marcie warmly. Freddie joined them all a second later, balancing a tea tray in her arms.

Marcie hurried to help the little girl with the tray. Now how did she manage to miss Freddie on the stairs? she wondered. Of course there remained the possibility that Freddie had taken another set of stairs up to the loft, found Marcie gone, and then come back downstairs. Marcie shrugged away the question, then turned to offer Jack some tea.

The man was no longer present.

After giving Marcie over to friendly folks, Jack set off to find the gruff Cole Coachman. He'd draw the man's cork should Cole not fashion to seek out Miss Marcie once Jack had had a word or two with him! Though Jack hardly approved of Miss Marcie's choice, he had to admit to himself that Cole Coachman had a certain air of respectability about him. But Jack was no fool. He knew that any man worth his salt needed to think there be a challenge in snaring the lady of his choice.

Jack met Cole Coachman just as Cole was stepping out of the library.

"Ho! You there," called Jack. "I would have a word with you, my fine coachman." Jack expected the man to turn away, but surprisingly he did not.

"Ah, Jack, my man," Cole Coachman greeted him. "Shall we commence to my buried coach together?"

Jack blinked in astonishment. Fancy that! Getting Cole Coachman alone proved to be a simpler feat than Jack had imagined.

"Lead the way, man," Jack said enthusiastically.

And the two of them headed out the front entrance of the vicarage, arm in arm, and looking as though they'd been friends for a lifetime.

Miss Deirdre, grinning, watched the two men head out the door. Her plans were already in motion. She was but one step away from having Jack as her own. Now, all that was left to be done was make certain Miss Marcie soon felt the gentle touch of one of Cupid's arrows.

Cole and Jack met Vicar Clarke, his orphan wards, and several of his male neighbors at the footbridge where the sled and its plow horse had been pulled to a halt. Jack made quick work of climbing into the sleigh, Cole following after. The incessant jangling of bells accompanied them as they made haste back to the main road.

Cole decided the moment would be as good as any to sway the uncouth Jack to courting the wily Miss Deirdre. Problem was, he didn't know quite how to phrase the suggestion.

In what he deemed a sorry attempt, he began: "Ah, Jack, my man, what think you of the lovely and . . . uh, available Miss Deirdre?"

Jack surprised his lordship by leaning back against a sturdy bale of hay that had been set down in the sled to be used later as traction beneath the carriage wheels. He grinned mightily.

"I think she be the sun that rises atop this sorry soul of mine. She be both angel and siren, and she be the one for ol' Jack here. Fact is, Cole Coachman, I intend to offer her me hand, that is, once we see to it your coach is set free of the snow and all."

Cole nearly choked on the chilling air coursing into his lungs. "You intend to ask her to marry you?" Cole asked, quite thunderstruck.

"Of course I do," answered Jack. "I be addled not to, seeing as how she's taken an interest in me and all."

"Now how the devil did you know she'd taken an interest in you?" demanded Cole, quite perplexed by it all.

"Why, she smiled at me just so. A man knows such things. And there be the matter of her warming to me once she'd had a chance to scratch old Bart's ears."

"Bart?" Cole said, quite exasperated. "Who the devil is *Bart?*"

"He be the sheepdog I done delivered years ago. A right sunny beast, always wagging his tail. Miss Deirdre took a liking to him straight away, she did."

"And so you knew then that she would accept your offer of marriage, did you?" asked Cole.

"That I did."

Cole rolled his eyes heavenward. Miss Deirdre had no need for a Cupid. As Cole saw it, the woman needed a protector from Jack's overeager pursuit.

"Now," said Jack, getting cosy in the hay and commencing to make a show of cleaning his fingernails with the blade of a knife, "I be thinking about yourself and the fine Miss Marcie."

"Oh?" said Cole.

"Aye," said Jack. "Miss Marcie be needing a firm hand in her life. I do declare you be that firm but gentle hand she needs."

"You don't say."

"I do at that."

They looked at each other, man to man, and Cole suddenly grew wary. "Are you perhaps playing matchmaker on Marcie's behalf?" asked Cole, a mite too anxiously.

Jack shook his head. "Never." And here he winked. "It was little Freddie's idea."

Cole frowned. "I thought as much."

"Miss Marcie might have asked it of me, but, of course, being the fine lady she be, she did no such thing." With that, Jack continued happily scraping away the dirt from beneath his fingernails.

Zounds, thought Cole. What an impossible conversation this was proving to be. He dismissed the idea of pumping the man for more information. The highwayman was obviously having some sport at the expense of Cole's feelings. Jack couldn't possibly know what was in Marcie's heart.

Or could he?

Cole suddenly turned back to the man. "Tell me all and tell me now," he demanded.

Jack raised one bushy eyebrow. "Ask me nicely and I might just tell all. Then again . . ." Jack allowed his voice to trail off.

Cole gritted his teeth. "For the love of God, man, has Marcie expressed an interest in me or not?"

Jack shrugged.

Cole balled his hands into fists. "Then tell me this: have I a prayer of winning her heart?"

"Perhaps," was Jack's cryptic reply.

"That's it?" Cole nearly shouted. "That's all you can say? Devil take it! Just what do you propose I do?"

"Be honest with her," Jack replied reasonably. "Tell her what's in your heart, that's all."

"That's it?" Cole demanded. "That is your advice?"

"Aye," said Jack, still cleaning his nails.

Cole fumed. His palm itched to yank the knife from Jack's thieving hands, place that same knife against Jack's neck and— *Egad,* thought Cole, *I am losing my mind.* Who among his friends of the ton, and himself included, would have ever imagined the stuffy Marquis of Sherringham harboring such thoughts?

Yet here he was, dressed as a coachman, bouncing along a snowy path in a decrepit sled, and his heart near to bursting with love for some runaway minx who claimed to be a miss of means! Too, he was actually considering doing bodily harm to an inept highwayman who had managed—where his lordship had not, damn it all!—to become a confidant of the fiery-haired runaway. It was all too preposterous, quite unbelievable, and not at all appropriate for the Marquis of Sherringham's stuffy life.

But that life, Cole soundly reminded himself, was far away at the moment. And though he did not wish to reject it totally, he did wish to return to Town a saner man—after all that was the very reason he'd taken on the running of the Royal Mail coach in the first place.

So thinking, Cole forced himself to relax and regain his composure. Gradually, he even managed to gather his thoughts. *Hm,* he thought to himself, *perhaps Jack is right. Perhaps I should confess to my Mistress Mischief and tell all.*

The very idea lifted a heavy, dark cloud from above him, and he began to feel a bit better. But the dilemma still remained, however, as to which truth should spill from his lips first to Marcie—that he loved her . . . or that he was, in fact, the Marquis of Sherringham and not the coachman he pretended to be.

Marcie, beset with jitters as to what Jack might or might not be doing, found she couldn't sit another minute within the cloying confines of the warm kitchen. She left the others to their cake-making, and hurried away in search of some solitude.

Unfortunately, she encountered the voluptuous Miss Deirdre in the hall.

"Marcie!" exclaimed Miss Deirdre. "You are the very one I had hoped to find!"

"I am?"

"Indeed. We have not yet had time to become better acquainted, you and I. Pity that, for I feel we have much in common. Come," said Miss Deirdre, leading the way to the sitting room.

It was Marcie's opinion that she and Miss Deirdre had little in common save the fact they were both more than a bit interested in the handsome Cole Coachman. Marcie, though, couldn't help but feel a certain curiosity about this female. She wished to learn for herself why Cole, Jack, and even the Prince Regent had become so smitten with the lady—all obvious physical reasons aside, of course—and so she followed the woman's lead.

The two were soon settled in the sitting room, whereupon Miss Deirdre commenced a brief and surprisingly touching explanation of her life's history.

She was the seventh daughter of nine born to an impoverished viscount and his lady. Her father, a man often in his cups, was given to verbally abusing both his wife and daughters, and it was the man's excessive need for drink and his subsequent tirades that finally forced Miss Deirdre to take drastic action.

What little respectability her birth gave her was soon lost when Miss Deirdre, at the tender age of fifteen, fled from beneath the severe hand of her drunken father and became mistress to a noble lord. A succession of peers soon followed, each of whom she claimed to have loved at the time she'd consented to become their mistress. Alas, she soon either learned of some hidden blemish in their characters or found their constant company to be quite boring after the first heat of passion faded fast away.

Though Miss Deirdre's life had been colorful, to say the least, she did not hesitate to point out that her chosen path in life had been unutterably lonely at times. Her father disowned her. Her sisters, those who chose to visit her on rare occasions, hid their faces behind heavy veils lest someone spy them paying a visit on a female of her class.

"Ah, but I am allowing my story to become quite dispiriting," said Miss Deirdre suddenly. "That was not my intent at all! Oh, I have suffered some trying moments, but all in all, I have been quite happy . . . that is, I thought I was happy. Until now."

Marcie was caught up in the woman's story. And truth to tell, she was rather impressed with Miss Deirdre's strong constitution. It was no secret that should a female not be blessed with connections or a healthy purse, she found herself at the mercy of "protectors."

Marcie had been saved from dire circumstances because her father had left her an independent heiress. God only knew what she'd have done had she been in Miss Deirdre's position.

"And what is it about the 'now' that has caused you to reassess your estimation of happiness?" asked Marcie.

Miss Deirdre gave a delicious sigh. "A man," she whispered. "I have met a man who has made me quite rethink my choices in life."

Marcie stiffened. She had no doubt who that man might be.

"I see," Marcie managed.

"I thought you would understand." Miss Deirdre leaned forward, clasping Marcie's hands in hers. "Dear me, but I have gone on at great length about my own self. Truly, that was not my intention. Here now, you must tell me about yourself, Marcie. Have you ever been in love?"

Marcie looked away, taking a deep breath. "Yes," she

said softly. *And unfortunately,* she thought, *the two of us have fallen in love with the same man!*

"Do tell," urged Miss Deirdre.

Marcie hesitated. She returned her gaze to the woman's lovely face. "Th—there isn't much to tell," she said truthfully. "The man hardly returns my sentiments."

"Oh?" replied Miss Deirdre, suddenly frowning. "Are you quite certain?"

"Quite."

"Hm . . . well," she muttered, looking utterly perplexed.

Marcie couldn't for the life of her deduce why the woman had become so tongue-tied. What could it possibly matter to Miss Deirdre if Marcie had fallen in love with a man who didn't return that love? Why, the woman looked positively upset!

Marcie sought to soothe. "Really," she insisted, "it is of little consequence. I suppose my heart shall soon mend." *But it will not,* Marcie added to herself.

Miss Deirdre eyed her closely. "There are other fish to fry, my dear."

"Beg pardon?" Marcie said.

"Take Cole Coachman—for example only, of course," Miss Deirdre added quickly.

"Of course," Marcie replied, feeling hurt the woman would toss his name into this impossible conversation.

"What woman would not wish to be by his side?" Miss Deirdre exclaimed. "Why, he is ever so handsome, not to mention handy with the reins and a veritable god along the roads. Why, I wouldn't even be surprised if he has connections higher up. He is quite the most magnificent man I have ever met!"

Marcie suddenly wished her chair would open up and swallow her whole. It pained her greatly to hear Miss Deirdre expound on Cole's qualities. Better the woman just took a knife and pierced it straight into Marcie's heart.

"Please," Marcie whispered.

But Miss Deirdre went on at great length singing Cole Coachman's praises.

Marcie began to feel physically ill, for now that she'd heard Miss Deirdre's tale, she felt a certain compassion for the woman. She could no longer despise Miss Deirdre for being overly beautiful and far too cunning when it came to matters of the male sex. The woman had had no choice but to make use of her fair face.

Still, Marcie could not help but remember the feel of Cole's lips pressing down over her own. How dare the man toy with her emotions while swaying the comely Miss Deirdre into his grasp?

Marcie shot to her feet. "Excuse me," she blurted, "but I—I must find my owl. I seem to have misplaced him."

Miss Deirdre sat back in her chair, stunned. "If you insist."

"I do," mumbled Marcie. She hastened toward the door, lifted the latch.

"Marcie?" called Miss Deirdre.

Marcie paused, but only because she'd come to like the too-lovely mistress of so many men. "Yes?" she said.

"This man you mentioned . . . are you truly in love with him?"

Marcie sucked in a deep, numbing breath. *God help me,* she thought, *but I love him more than life itself.* To Miss Deirdre, she whispered, "Yes. I am truly in love with him."

"Then let him go," said Miss Deirdre. "And if he returns, then he is yours. If he does not, then he never was yours. Do you understand what I am saying?"

Marcie bit her lip, holding her tears at bay. "I think I do," she whispered.

And then she thrust the door open and hastened away.

Cole returned to the vicarage much the worse for wear. His coach was now freed, thanks to the vicar's neighbors, and was positioned down near the footbridge. Cole, running one hand through his wet hair, went in search of Miss Deirdre. He found her in the sitting room, gazing out a window. "Well?" he asked, after closing the door soundly behind him.

Miss Deirdre bolted out of her chair. "Cole! What a fright you look."

"Forget that," he said. "What of Miss Marcie? Had you a moment to speak with her?"

Miss Deirdre frowned. "I did," she said. "I am sorry, Cole, but she seems to have fallen completely in love with someone else!"

"Who?" he demanded.

Miss Deirdre shook her head. "I haven't a clue, but I can tell you the man does not return her favor. Oh, it is a sad story, to be certain, but there you have it. Miss Marcie is most definitely in love, Cole."

Cole batted his coachman's hat against his leg. "Damn!" he muttered. "I had thought, during that moment we shared at the bridge, that the two of us had come to an understanding. I had thought . . . well, it doesn't much matter, does it?"

Miss Deirdre moved to touch his sleeve with a soft caress. "I am sorry, Cole. I did my best to cast you in a favorable light. But she loves another."

Cole's eyes turned stormy. "B'gad," he muttered passionately. "I would like nothing better than to wring the man's neck with my bare hands!"

"Oh, pray, don't!" cried Miss Deirdre. "You would succeed only in further cleaving her heart in two! Ah, Cole, but she is so young and impressionable. Perhaps she shall soon forget the man? Perhaps, if you made your intentions known, she would turn her thoughts to you?"

Cole stiffened. "I will not be second choice," he said. "Never again." And here, he thought of the brothers he'd lost, and how he'd been second to them in their father's eyes.

No! Cole would never, ever be second best again. And certainly not with Marcie. He wished to capture her heart totally, not to play second fiddle to some faceless being.

Cole drew himself up to his full height, and, suddenly, he was no longer simply Cole Coachman but the titled swell, the Marquis of Sherringham. Cole Coachman was no more.

Miss Deirdre drew back, clearly recognizing the change in him.

"My lord," she whispered, "please do not judge her too harshly."

Cole glanced over at the woman. "I shall not judge her at all," he said, emotionless. "I shall simply deliver her to the inn at Burford and then . . . ah, then," he whispered, "I will be rid of the mischievous miss and her confounded bird once and for all."

His words caused a prick of pain to target directly into his heart. Cole ignored the piercing pain; he knew it only too well. He lifted the latch of the door, intending to leave the vicarage and never again set eyes upon it.

But Miss Deirdre's soft cries stayed him.

Cole turned to look over one shoulder at her. "Surely you are not shedding tears for Miss Marcie and me," he said, sounding for all the world like the peer of the realm he was.

Miss Deirdre stiffened. "No," she said, brazenly. "I am crying for what might have been. The tears I shed are for Marcie, and for the Cole Coachman she thought she knew."

" 'Tis a waste," replied Cole. "Cole Coachman and his Mistress Mischief never had a chance. The two were woefully mismatched. Two such wayward souls were trouble in triplicate from the moment they met."

Miss Deirdre lifted her chin. "And if I told you I think not, my lord? What would you do?"

Cole shook his head, laughing the cutting laugh he'd too often laughed while in Town. "I'd say you were wrong, my dear."

"But ofttimes two odds make even," offered Miss Deirdre, not backing down.

Cole's grin turned rueful. "Sometimes," he admitted. "Take you and Jack, for instance." He heard the catch of her breath, then continued, "Yes, Miss Deirdre. Jack is quite enamored of you. Indeed, you had no need of a Cupid at all. Jack intends to make an offer for you."

Miss Deirdre, stunned, said nothing.

"I wish you well," Cole said, meaning the words.

"Thank you," murmured Miss Deirdre.

Cole, however, had already turned on his heel and left the room. He had no wish to witness the true face of love firsthand. It smarted to realize that his Mistress Mischief had set her sights for another. God, what a fool he'd been, falling in love with Marcie!

And a fool he remained.

But no one would know of the fact. No one, save himself, he vowed.

Thirteen

Marcie paid her respects to the vicar, his wife, and their charges before she headed for the Mail coach outside. Saying good-bye to Freddie, however, proved difficult indeed. Marcie knelt down beside the little orphan girl, who was, quite obviously, doing her best not to cry.

Marcie lovingly brushed one bouncy brown curl behind the girl's ear. "I shall miss you most of all, Freddie," she whispered. "You would not mind if I came back to visit, would you?"

Freddie's eyes widened with anticipation. "Oh, Miss Marcie, that would make me ever so happy!"

Marcie smiled. "It would make me happy, too. I shall return just as soon as I . . . as soon as I decide where I shall be living."

"Oh, dear! You have no home?" Freddie's brow wrinkled with worry.

Marcie hastened to ease the girl's concern. "Of course I do," she replied. "I have many homes, actually," she added.

Marcie thought of her godmama's invitation to take up residence at Stormhaven. Too, she could live for a while with Mirabella and her handsome husband, the Earl of Blackwood. And, of course, her other cousin, Meredith, would certainly take her in. Also, there was always the possibility of returning to St. Ives. But though Marcie had loved living in the West Country, she did not truly wish to return there now that her father was gone. Lastly, there remained the matter of agreeing to be courted by some stuffy Marquis of Sherringham her cousins had chosen as a perfect parti for her. . . .

The latter thought did not inspire Marcie. Indeed, the idea of becoming wife to any man other than Cole Coachman seemed not only abhorrent but deceitful as well. Marcie sighed.

Little Freddie, perhaps reading Marcie's meandering thoughts, took that moment to throw her arms about Marcie's neck. She hugged her tightly.

"Don't you fret, Miss Marcie," whispered the little girl into Marcie's ear. "I have made a very special wish, for you and for me. I have decided that the fossils you gave me will be my wishing rocks. Tonight I shall rub them each three times and say my wishes aloud. Can you guess what I've wished?"

Marcie shook her head.

"That you shall marry your coachman," Freddie whispered.

A moment passed.

"And—and for yourself, Freddie?" Marcie managed to whisper.

Freddie's arms tightened even more about Marcie's neck. "For a family," she said with all the candor of youth. "For a mama just like you, and for a father as nice as your coachman."

Marcie shut her eyes tight, pressed her face against Freddie's soft, fragrant curls. How sweet the girl was. How very precious.

Marcie knew, in that instant, what she would do once she'd decided where to take up residence. She had the funds to take care of Freddie. She had a wellspring of love to give the orphan. The only thing she could not offer the girl was "a father as nice as Cole Coachman."

Marcie gently drew out of the hug. She brushed one gloved hand lovingly along Freddie's pretty jaw. "I will be back," she promised.

Freddie nodded. "I believe you," she whispered. Her tiny face lit with a warm and trusting smile.

There came, suddenly, the sound of Cole Coachman's call. He was ready to leave.

The Cole Coachman Marcie encountered while heading with her owl towards the Mail coach was not the Cole Coachman she remembered. This man, while still as brusque and impatient as Cole ever could be, was exceedingly cold in both manner and voice. Indeed, he seemed determined not to demonstrate any emotion whatsoever toward her, save one of extreme disinterest. Marcie, while hurt to the quick, made a grand show of displaying neither her displeasure nor her disappointment.

The fact that Jack took up the hind boot, in placement of John Reeve, and that Miss Deirdre insisted on perching herself there beside the man, only added to Marcie's miserable mood, and seemed quite ridiculous. Now why in the deuce was Miss Deirdre fawning over Jack? wondered Marcie. But she need only hear Cole Coachman bark an order to one and all to hurry and board, adding sharply that he hadn't all day to tarry at the vicarage; obviously, Miss Deirdre, so accustomed to men addressing her in tender tones, had come to the conclusion that Cole Coachman was a bit too rough around the edges to suit her taste. Heavens, but the woman seemed to fall in and out of love with lightning speed! If only she herself possessed such an ability, thought

Marcie, gazing up at Jack, who was sharing some private words with Miss Deirdre.

"Mistress! If you please, step inside the coach. I've parcels to deliver and I fear you are holding us up."

Marcie blinked, yanking her thoughts back to the present at the sound of Cole Coachman's brusque tone.

Her eyes met his, and the sight she beheld chilled her to the bone. His eyes were as wintry gray as they had been that first moment she'd met him. He glared at her as though he wished he'd never had the misfortune of crossing her path.

Marcie's heart grew queerly tight. She felt the hot prick of tears threatening to overwhelm her. Damn him, she thought angrily. Damn him for his moody ways . . . and damn herself for loving him.

Marcie straightened, fought back the tears. "You needn't snap at me," she replied, her voice just as clipped as his.

"And I could say the same to you, Mistress."

Oh! thought Marcie, *but the man can be perfectly maddening!* Her face burned with both anger and embarrassment as she remembered how she had thrown caution to the wind and allowed him to kiss her. But what hurt her more was the fact that she had fallen helplessly and hopelessly in love with the mercurial coachman. Even now, she could remember the taste and feel of his mouth on hers, could recall the warmth of his embrace. . . .

Enough, Marcie firmly scolded herself. The man clearly wanted nothing more to do with her. She had too much pride to allow herself to grovel at his feet.

So thinking, she said, "Though I have proved to be a perfect nuisance to you during our travels, I assure you I shall not be the cause of any further disasters."

The words came too strongly from her lips, and Marcie

immediately regretted the sharp tone of her voice. But she couldn't help herself.

"Famous," he said, his sarcasm not lost on Marcie. "I shall hold you to that promise. Now, if you please?" He nodded toward the carriage door, clearly impatient to be done with the conversation and to see that she was safely tucked inside, out of his way.

Marcie spun away from him, so close to tears that she feared she would make a cake of herself should she remain in his presence a moment longer. That he had the sheer audacity to help her mount the steps threw her senses into complete confusion. His touch was warm and far too familiar. She felt his searing heat through her pelisse and the sleeve of her gown. It proved, alas, too much for her to bear.

Marcie pulled away from him so abruptly that Prinny, perched on her shoulder, grew restless. She immediately sought to soothe the bird, but Bart chose that moment to come barreling down upon the coach, barking all the while. The dog came tearing round the coach, frightening not only the horses but the owl as well.

Prinny rustled his feathers.

Bart, spying the bird, leapt up from the ground and gave a happy bark as he pounced against Marcie. She cried out as she was forced against the coach. Cole Coachman muttered a sharp expletive. And Prinny, injured wing and all, took flight into the air, heading for the trees. Marcie tried to stop the bird, but Bart, all tongue and paws, fastened her against the coach.

"Prinny!" Marcie cried.

But it was too late. The bird was gone.

Cole Coachman hauled the dog off her. "Down, dammit!" he yelled.

Bart heeled, plopping himself down on the ground and then stared up at the coachman expectantly.

Marcie watched as her owl lost himself in the copse near the bridge.

"He is gone," she whispered. And suddenly the events of the day proved to be too much. Her tears came freely.

Bart licked at her gloved hands, whimpering softly. Marcie, quite overwrought, found she could do nothing more than kneel down and try to hide her tears in the soft fur of the dog.

"Blast," muttered Cole Coachman. "Do not cry. I shall go in search of your owl. I'll find him and—"

"No!" Marcie shook her head. "You—you have your parcels to deliver. I would not wish to delay you more than I have. Besides, Prinny was never mine to begin with."

Marcie dashed her tears away, lifted her face to Cole Coachman's. Ah, how handsome he appeared with the snow a sharp contrast to his dark good looks. And if she didn't know better, she would have thought that his gray eyes had softened somewhat in the past few seconds. Why, those gray orbs were almost as tender as she remembered them during the moment he'd kissed her. Marcie decided this was the way in which she wanted to remember her Cole Coachman, the one with whom she'd fallen so helplessly in love.

"Let him go," she whispered to Cole Coachman.

"But you have become quite fond of the bird. I thought you wished to keep him."

"I did wish to keep him. But I—I told you once that I have found life to be a series of meetings and partings." She tipped a rueful smile up at Cole Coachman. "Prinny's leaving is just one more parting I must learn to accept. I fear I am learning that lesson all too well."

Cole Coachman frowned. He helped her to her feet.

Marcie, murmuring her thanks, fought not to make too much of his attentions. He was being kind, nothing more. She must remember that. Marcie turned away, intending to climb into the carriage.

Cole's words stopped her. "I cannot just leave this place—not without attempting to retrieve your owl."

Marcie glanced over her shoulder at Cole, and her heart verily broke at the handsome sight of him. She shook her head, staying him from leaving his coach in search of the owl.

"A friend once told me that should I love something—or someone—I should let them go free. If they return, then they are mine, and if they do not. . . ." She let her words trail off as she looked out at the copse of trees. "I shall let Prinny go free," she said softly. And then, returning her gaze to Cole, she said, "As for you, Cole Coachman, you've Valentine parcels to deliver, have you not? I suggest you get this coach moving." With that, Marcie straightened her shoulders and climbed into the carriage.

She did not relax until Cole Coachman had folded up the steps and closed the door behind her. Only then did she press gloved hands against her face and cry openly.

Cole felt a perfect beast. Gad, what had made him bark at the lovely miss? Why the devil had he been so abrupt with Miss Marcie when what he wanted to do was take her in his arms and kiss her soundly?

No doubt the reason was because he loved her, wanted to make her his wife. Yet, she loved another—a man who did not return her love.

Cole blew out an exasperated breath and headed for his bench. He could not calm the roiling of his own emotions.

The fact that Marcie had addressed him as "Cole Coachman," and not "My Lord Monarch," pained him no small amount. He had quite obviously come to the end of the road with his Mistress Mischief.

Cole clenched his jaw tight. He whipped his team into motion, heading for the open road and for the inn at Burford.

Inside the coach, Marcie watched as the vicarage became smaller and smaller and then was soon lost behind the very line of trees Prinny had fled toward. Marcie felt a horrible sense of loss. She'd not only lost Prinny but the Cole Coachman she'd come to love as well.

The fact that she was surrounded by all kinds of Saint Valentine's Day gifts destined for sweethearts, loved ones, and lovers in the Cotswolds did nothing to ease Marcie's sadness. She glanced around the interior of the coach, seeing small packages and large, all beautifully wrapped in varying shades of reds and pinks and, no doubt, containing bottles of scent, pretty bonnets, or perhaps some expensive lace purchased in the finest shops in London. Her eyes misted with more tears.

It was Saint Valentine's Day, but instead of feeling the pleasant heat of one of Cupid's arrows piercing into her soul, she felt as though her heart had been shattered into a thousand pieces. The sting of unrequited love burned through her. *Oh, Cole,* she thought, *why couldn't things have turned out differently for us? Why could you not love me as much as I do you?*

Marcie's only comfort was in knowing that soon, very soon, she would return to the vicarage and make the needed preparations to adopt Freddie, and perhaps even Masters Neville and Theodore as well. But alas, this plan, too, proved lacking, for she could not yet give the children the father little Freddie dreamed of having one day. Marcie began to cry anew.

"I just knew it." It was Nan speaking.

Marcie snapped her head toward Nan, who was, as usual, perched amidst a pile of packages.

"Nan. Pray, forgive me for crying. I . . . I am just overly tired."

"Fustian," Nan muttered. "I've no doubt but your sweet heart has been abused by Cole. No, do not try and tell me otherwise," said Nan when Marcie opened her mouth in protest. "I have known Cole a long time. A *very* long time. I know what a beast he can be. I tell you now, I intend to have a word or two with him. Mark my words, Cole's ears will burn with shame once I've had my say."

Marcie gave her friend a horrified look. "No," she gasped. "Just let it be, Nan. I have no wish for you to speak to Cole on my behalf. I—I am crying because I lost my owl and—"

"And you are lying," cut in Nan, harrumphing soundly. She folded her arms across her chest and stewed. "Cole has ever been a thick-headed bore—save the moments when he was driving a coach along the open roads, and, of course, save the few moments when he actually let his guard down and allowed himself to enjoy the freshness of your company. Do not let him fool you, Marcie. He is just so very insufferable at times, but I know him and I know that he has enjoyed your company."

"What he wishes," corrected Marcie, "is that he never set eyes on me."

"I cannot believe such a thing."

"Well you'd best face the fact, Nan. I have proved to be nothing but a thorn in his side. He—he despises me."

"On the contrary, I think he has fallen in love with you."

"You, dear friend, are confusing compassion with love." Marcie thrust herself back against the squabs and studiously stared out the window. "I no longer wish to discuss our coachman. The only thing I wish is that he deliver me safely to the inn at Burford . . . and that I get beyond this blasted holiday of hearts and flowers, and . . . and love."

"Oh, Marcie," whispered Nan. "To hear you, of all people, say such a thing about Saint Valentine's Day is sad indeed. From the moment I met you amid the book stalls, I knew I'd finally found a kindred spirit who loved romance as much as I do."

"On the contrary," Marcie said, "I've since learned romance is not the wondrous thing so many poets hope to make young women believe it is."

Nan looked as though she was about to shed a few tears herself. "If I can't change your opinion about love, perhaps I can sway you in your choice of stopping at Burford. Please, do not say that you've decided not to travel on to your godmama's home. You said yourself your cousins have found you a perfect parti in the form of some fine, titled swell."

"Haven't you heard a word I've said, Nan? I'm not looking for courtship, or even love. And I've certainly no need of a titled gent. I've blunt enough of my own to do as I please."

"And what might that be?" Nan asked, wary.

Marcie hadn't a clue. What she wanted to do was turn back the hands of time to the moment when Cole Coachman had held her close and kissed her. What she wanted, was for Cole to pledge his love for her, and she for him. To dance with him at the Valentine's ball her godmama was no doubt planning. She wanted to dance the night away in his warm embrace, to have him guide her around a candlelit ballroom. What she wanted, blast it all, was to share a life with Cole . . . a life that included the orphans she'd come to care for and, God willing, children she and Cole would create. . . .

She drew in a ragged sigh. Silly dreams. That's what her thoughts were. Dreams that would never, ever come true.

"Please, Nan," Marcie begged, suddenly weary. "Do not speak to me of Cole Coachman. He has made it quite clear he wants nothing more to do with me. I just—I wish to spend the remaining miles with my eyes closed and my mind empty." Marcie leaned her head against the cushions and forced her eyes closed.

"Wait," pressed Nan.

Marcie opened one eye. "Wait for what?"

Nan fidgeted. "Just promise me that you'll reconsider traveling to your godmama's home. After all, Marcie, it isn't every day that a girl has the chance of capturing the interest of a marquis. And since you've chosen not to pursue our coachman, well, you must promise me at least to consider the Marquis of Sherringham."

"Nan, I just told you I'm not—"

"I know what you told me. I also know *you,* Marcie. You need love in your life, and laughter, and to be surrounded with tender hearts, and flowering blooms, and all of God's creatures. Please. Promise me you'll at least give the marquis a chance. Who knows? He may be the man to bring such things to you. Meet him. That's all I ask."

Marcie let out a long breath.

"Promise me," insisted Nan.

Marcie thought the girl too swayed by romantic melodrama. But Nan's request had been too heartfelt not to be considered. "Very well," Marcie said, knowing her friend was only trying to help and seeing no other recourse. Nan would no doubt plague her to death if she didn't relent. "I promise to meet the man. Now, will you leave me be?"

Nan nodded, complacent at last.

And Marcie, finally left to her own miserable thoughts, fell into a restless slumber. Her dreams were filled with visions of Cole's wintry gaze, his haunting smile, and memories of his lips pressed against hers. And she dreamed of the sweet nothings Cole would never whisper into her ear. Though she knew she should open her eyes and stop tormenting herself with such visions, she couldn't. She didn't want to. Marcie knew she'd spend the rest of her life dreaming of Cole. For only in her dreams, would he truly be hers.

Marcie didn't come awake until she felt the coach rattle to a halt in the coachyard of the inn at Burford. It was time to say a final farewell to her monarch of the road.

Cole, having charged his team along the snowy roads, frowned at sight of the inn. There came a rush of folk hastening toward the coach once he'd pulled his horses to a halt within the wide courtyard. Cole barked the usual orders, was rewarded with two early flowering crocuses found somewhere amid the snow by a fetching maid, and was soon swept up into a frenzy of activity. He oversaw the unpacking of parcels meant for the busy inn, as well as the change of his horses. Fortunately, the bulk of the packages were destined for this station.

He was just unlashing a keg of ale, an action meant merely to keep his miserable thoughts at bay, when Marcie and Nan alighted the coach. Cole wished he could be the one to help Marcie down the steps, but Jack was awarded the chance to make that gentlemanly gesture. He watched as Marcie gave the highwayman a kiss on the cheek and a warm hug, obviously saying farewell to her friend.

Cole felt the unholy urge to toss Jack into a snowbank. He pulled too hard on the barrel, breaking the lash that held it in place, and nearly toppled himself onto his backside. He managed to catch his balance just as Marcie moved toward him.

Embarrassed that she'd nearly seen him fall on his rump, he slammed the barrel onto the ground, then glared in her direction.

"What's the trouble now?" he demanded. Gad, but he was being snappish. But he couldn't help himself. He loved her. And she, blast her, loved another.

Marcie stood rigidly before him. "I meant only to pay you for your trouble, sir," she said, emphasizing the last word.

To Cole's dismay, she pulled a small purse out from her pocket and began to count out an exorbitant sum. Cole blanched.

"Good God!" he uttered. "Where in the devil did you come by such a sum of coin? Do not tell me you won it in that ridiculous dice game miles ago!"

"Certainly not," Marcie replied, clearly miffed. "As I tried to tell you once, I am, in fact, a miss of means." She thrust the bundle of coin toward him. "Go on. Take it. Consider it payment for your countless troubles in seeing me safely to my destination."

Cole paled. A miss of means? When would she cease this jest of hers? And the coins—where the devil had she gotten them? He doubted Marcie had had this sum of money on her person when he'd first met her at the mews for if she had, she need not have bothered to steal a ride with Nan.

"Put it away," Cole demanded. "I've no need to take your coin. No doubt you will need it in the future."

"I assure you, Cole Coachman," Miss Marcie said, her words coming fast and clipped, "I've a fountain of blunt to see me not only through my lifetime but that of three generations of descendants as well. Now take what I offer you so that I may be once and for all truly done with you."

Cole, tired of the mischievousness that had led him to fall in love with her, turned away from the sight of her beauteous face. He'd be damned if he'd take so much as a half penny from her. That he had to leave her at all was painful enough, but to rob her of her coin as well? He wouldn't do it.

Cole reached for yet another keg lashed to the coach. Again, he pulled too hard. This time, however, the barrel split a seam, and a gush of ale came spilling down to cover his shiny boots.

"Damn you!" he shouted at the barrel, truly vexed.

Marcie managed to dart out of the way of spilled ale, but Cole heard her cry of anguish nonetheless.

"And damn *you,* Cole Coachman!" she gasped, choking on tears. She threw down the bag of coin and then scurried away.

Cole swung round. "Wait!" he called, meaning to stop her and explain that he'd not been damning *her* but the barrel.

But his tearing of the keg from the hind boot resulted in a veritable flood of more barrels, frozen hams, crates of imported oranges, and boxes filled with mincemeat pies from the best pastry houses in London tumbling down upon him. Cole found himself caught beneath an avalanche of goods. A heavy barrel hit him full on the shin. A heavy ham slammed down upon his chest, and several oranges, spilling free of their crate, hit him squarely atop his coachman's hat. Cole, fastened to the ground beneath the goods, could only groan in angry frustration.

"Need a hand, mate?" said a too familiar voice from above him. It was Jack, standing arm-in-arm with Miss Deirdre, the two of them peering down at him.

Cole growled deep in his throat. "Don't just stand there, man! Get that blasted barrel off me!"

Jack hastened to oblige while Miss Deirdre shook her head at Cole.

"Ah, Cole," she whispered sadly. "Why ever did you shout at Marcie so? You've completely frightened your miss away."

Cole didn't need Miss Deirdre to tell him that. He got to his feet, with Jack's help, and watched as Marcie, eyes filled with tears, turned at the doorway of the inn to glance one last time in his direction.

Her eyes were just as lovely as he remembered. But her mouth, so pouty and full, was turned down. Their eyes met and held for a fraction of a second, and then she turned away from him and hurried into the inn.

Cole felt as though the sun had just slipped forever behind a dark and ominous cloud.

Nan, having followed Marcie into the inn, tried unsuccessfully to sway her friend's emotions toward Cole.

"Cole Coachman isn't always so horrid," offered Nan. "He can be quite a gentleman. Oh, please, Marcie, do not judge Cole so harshly. I am certain he will deliver you to your godmama's home if only we ask him to do so."

Marcie shook the snow from her pelisse, motioning for one of the maids. "I've no further need of your Cole Coachman," she said. "I intend to hire a local conveyance to take me to Stormhaven."

"Cole will take you there."

Marcie's lips tightened. "He's manning a Royal Mail coach not a stage coach! And besides Cole Coachman has made it quite clear he wishes to be done with me. I've granted him that wish. I have paid him in full for his troubles."

"Cole has no need of your money, Marcie. Oh, please, just say you will allow him to take you to Stormhaven."

Marcie shook her head. "I have made my decision, Nan." She commenced to give her instructions to the maid now beside her. The maid informed her that a wagon of goods was even now being readied to travel into Stow-on-the-Wold, and also to the nearby Stormhaven.

Marcie asked the maid to inquire if there might be room for her aboard the wagon.

Nan frowned. "So you are giving up on Cole Coachman, are you? Does this mean you've decided to take up your cousins' offer of introducing you to the Marquis of Sherringham?"

Marcie, not forgetting her promise to Nan, nodded. Besides, she was too tired to argue again about consenting to consider some stuffy marquis.

"Well, then, I guess this is good-bye for now."

"It would seem so," said Marcie. She turned toward her friend, giving her a warm hug. "I'll not forget you, Nan. Let us promise to keep in touch."

They hugged each other tight for a moment, and then, when the maid returned with news that Marcie could indeed find a ride to Stormhaven, they parted company.

Marcie watched as Nan headed out the inn door. She wouldn't cry, she told herself. She wouldn't. But as the latch dropped into place, and as she imagined Nan scurrying for the Mail coach—and Cole—Marcie's tears fell unchecked.

It would be a very, very long time before Marcie would be able to forget Cole Coachman. Indeed, Marcie admitted to herself, she knew she would *never* forget him.

Cole saw Nan returning to the coach. "That was a quick good-bye," he said. *Too quick,* Cole thought. Though the parcels had been unloaded, he felt somehow unsettled, as though he'd left something undone. No doubt it was because he had not had the chance to say a proper farewell to his Mistress Mischief.

As for Jack and Miss Deirdre, the two would be staying on at the inn for an indefinite time.

"I've decided to turn over a new leaf in life," Miss Deirdre explained to Cole, as Jack unpacked the last of her baggage. Miss Deirdre's voice dropped a note as she said, "Jack and I will soon be married."

Cole shook his head, not a little amazed. "You must love him very much to give up your life of luxury."

Miss Deirdre nodded. "I do love him . . . but I'll not be giving up any luxuries."

"Pray do not tell me Jack has encouraged you to join him in his highwayman's antics!"

"Certainly not," said Miss Deirdre, crinkling her nose. "You shall be the first to know that I have decided to write my memoirs. I am certain there are those among the ton who would pay a handsome price to ensure their names do not appear in print."

"Ah," said Cole. "I see." And then he laughed, very glad

that Miss Deirdre had at last found happiness. He had little doubt but that her memoirs would prove vastly entertaining.

Miss Deirdre gave him a rueful smile in return. "I wish things had turned out differently for you and Marcie."

"As do I!" It was Jack who said the words. Having finished unloading Miss Deirdre's baggage, he'd come to stand beside her and was now looking at Cole with an accusing glare. "You be a fool not to go after the girl, Cole Coachman."

Cole did not argue with the man; he was thinking the same thing. But Marcie was exactly where she'd wanted to be. He had brought her to Burford, just as he'd promised. All that was left to do was to get on with his life.

Cole tipped his hat in a final farewell to both Jack and Miss Deirdre, then motioned for Nan to sit with him on the box. He had no desire to ride alone. Not now.

They'd no sooner headed out of the courtyard than Nan skewered Cole with an angry glare.

"How could you?" she cried.

"How could I what?"

"Abuse Marcie in such a way?"

"Abuse her?" Cole said. *"Me* abuse *her?* Devil take it, Nan, but thoughts of Marcie have haunted me this entire ride!"

"And did you tell her so?" Nan demanded.

"T-tell her?" Cole asked. "Well, no, of course not. How could I? She is clearly in love with another man. How could I confess my thoughts while she pines for another?"

"Oh!" moaned Nan, quite theatrically. "What a perfect fool you have been, Cole. There *is* no other man. Marcie loves you! She's loved you from the first, yet you thwarted her at every step."

"What the devil are you saying, Nan?"

Nan waved one hand in the air. "No matter. You still have a chance to make things right. She is, after all, the heiress your sisters-in-law have arranged for you to meet."

At that, Cole hauled his team to a stop. *"What?"* he yelled.

Nan cowered. "Now don't go getting angry with me," she gasped. "I knew all along that Marcie was the heiress for you, and you the titled swell meant for her. But I thought it would be best to let the two of you get better acquainted along the road. Oh, Cole, do not glare at me as though you'd like nothing better than to see me hanged! You know yourself what a crosspatch you've become since ascending to the title. As for Marcie, why she is far too spirited to agree to marry a stuffy marquis! And I just thought . . . well, I thought you and Marcie could have some fun together during this Mail ride. Could get to know each other."

Cole gaped at her. "Marcie is the heiress my sisters-in-law have been sputtering about? *She* is the one I've been dreading to meet?"

"Y—yes," admitted Nan.

"And you didn't tell me?" Cole roared.

Nan winced. "How could I? Lord, Cole, but you've been known to make even a titled heiress cry! I didn't want you thinking Marcie was one of those hen-witted heiresses you'd dealt with in the past. And I didn't want Marcie believing you were some stuffy swell whose company she must endure. I wanted the two of you to meet on even ground. I wanted you to see what a treat Marcie is, and I wanted, blast you, for Marcie to see that the Marquis of Sherringham isn't always a such a complete bore!"

Cole couldn't believe what he was hearing. Marcie was the heiress he'd been trying to avoid? And he was the stuffy swell she'd been doing her best to steer clear of? Good God. What a mess.

"Nan," he muttered, "I should throttle you."

"But you won't."

"And how can you be so certain?" he demanded.

"Because," said Nan, with utter certainty, "you are no longer the Cole Coachman or the Marquis of Sherringham I remember."

"And how can you be so sure of that?"

"Because the both of them would have boxed my ears by now."

"I may just do exactly that!"

Nan shook her head. "I doubt it," she assured him. "You see, Cole, or Sherry, or whatever it is you've become, you are not the same person you were when starting out on this journey and you know it. Marcie has changed you."

"Do not be ridiculous."

"I'm not," Nan replied. "Now turn left, down this road."

"What?"

"Left!" Nan called, reaching to help guide the reins.

The coach bumped over a rut in the snowy road, then rattled onward.

Nan smiled up at her half brother. "You want to be at Stormhaven soon after Marcie arrives, don't you?" she asked. "Well, since you must take me to my mother's uncle's house in Stow and you still must deliver the last of your parcels there, then you should at least stop at Stormhaven and let them know you have every intention of joining them as soon as possible. If my calculations are correct, we should be there well before Marcie."

Cole, damning the consequences of this irregular run of the Royal Mails, for once in his life, did not argue.

Fourteen

The transformation of one Marcelon Victoria Darlington from a mischievous West Country girl into a refined young lady destined to capture the heart of a titled gentleman began that very late afternoon upon Marcie's arrival at Stormhaven.

Marcie arrived at her godmama's home cold and wrinkled from her trek aboard a creaky old wagon—a wagon filled with extra goods for her godmama's Saint Valentine's Day ball. The ball was to be the culmination of Penelope Barrington's seven-day house party in honor of Saint Valentine, and it was set to take place that very evening. But though Marcie was much travel-worn and most likely looked a fright, her beautiful cousins, Mirabella and Meredith, swept her into warm hugs. Even her godmama, the outlandish Penelope Barrington, known for her eccentric ways, paid no mind to Marcie's bedraggled appearance.

Nor were her cousins or Aunt Nellie—as she and her cousins called Penelope—aghast to hear that Marcie had run away from her boarding school. They were, however, most upset that Marcie had endured the cruelties of the switch-wielding Mistress Cheltenham. They assured Marcie that, had she but hinted at her unhappiness, they would have hastened to Town to retrieve her from that horrible school.

Aunt Nellie, clamping between her teeth a teakwood pipe—the bowl of which depicted two naked lovers entwined in a most shocking position—declared that she would soon pay a personal visit to one Betina Cheltenham.

Marcie couldn't help but smile. Ah, what she wouldn't give to be a fly on the wall when the indomitable Penelope Barrington cut the nasty Mistress Cheltenham down to size! Marcie regretted that she'd been too stubborn to turn to her family for help, and she told Aunt Nellie as much when the older woman asked why Marcie hadn't alerted them.

Marcie shook her head, frowning. "It was because I was determined to carry out my father's dying wish that I become a lady. He'd so wanted me to go to London and enroll in Mistress Cheltenham's School for Young Ladies, and though I'd fought him tooth and nail for so long, I found I had to do just that after his death." Marcie sighed. "Had my father known of Mistress Cheltenham's true nature, he never would have made arrangements for me to go to her."

"Certainly not," agreed Aunt Nellie. She gave Marcie's hand a squeeze. "But here now, let us forget this evil headmistress. You've become a beautiful young lady despite the woman's harshness."

"Hardly," said Marcie. "I fear I have yet to acquire the gentle ways of true lady. In fact, I'd rather don a pair of breeches and climb the nearest tree than suffer a moment in some gown with too tight sleeves."

"Bravo for you, my dear," said Aunt Nellie. "Breeches are all the rage for ladies in some countries, did you know? And climbing trees does wonders for a woman's figure."

"Auntie!" gasped the amber-eyed and soft-spoken Meredith. "Pray, do not encourage her wild nature. Marcie should have the chance to hone her finer sensibilities."

Aunt Nellie harrumphed loudly. "There is something to be said for breeches, my dear Merry. Did I not tell you of the time I donned buckskins and helped scout out a herd of buffalo in the American west? I had need of tree climbing then, my sweet."

Meredith sighed in exasperation.

Marcie giggled, for she could indeed imagine her eccentric godmama, dressed now in a creation of flowing watered silks, and a stunning turquoise turban winking with diamonds, donning buckskins and climbing trees.

"As you can see," Meredith whispered to Marcie, "Aunt Nellie hasn't changed a bit. She remains as unorthodox as you no doubt remember her."

"I am glad," said Marcie, warmed by the wink Aunt Nellie sent in her direction.

The blond-haired Mirabella joined the conversation. "Take care, Marcie," warned she good-naturedly, "lest you'll find yourself yearning to travel to parts unknown alongside her. Aunt Nellie has been busy these many years past, what with all her worldly jaunts, not to mention several marriages in between."

Aunt Nellie leaned toward Marcie. "Take my advice, dear girl, and marry a strapping young gentleman who hasn't one foot in the grave. I can't for the life of me manage to keep a husband alive for longer than a tour. Now mind you, the duke I wed just two years ago seemed for all the world to be as healthy as an ox, but he—God rest his wondrous soul—let go his final breath while we were hunting in India. Not only had I the trouble of carting home his trophy heads but his once lusty body to boot!"

Marcie tried to keep her giggles in check, but she couldn't help herself and was soon laughing alongside Mirabella and Meredith as Aunt Nellie commenced to recount her troubles of obtaining not only a berth for her dead husband's guns and trophies, but also having to insist at every border that the coffin her servants bore was not filled with ivory tusks but her husband himself.

"Oh!" exclaimed Mirabella, "all this talk of being a lady and marrying a healthy gentleman has just reminded me that the Marquis of Sherringham paid his respects not an hour ago. Claimed he had some business to attend to but that he'd return for the banquet. Zeus and Minerva, Marcie! I'd quite forgotten that Merry and I promised to introduce you to his lordship."

"Oh, yes," exclaimed Meredith. "We must get you upstairs and see you gowned in the first stare of fashion. Whatever have we been thinking to tarry so long?"

Marcie was quick to explain that she had no desire to meet any peer of the realm. She wasn't ready by far to meet such a gentleman, she said, adding to herself that she wasn't of a mind to try and entice any man—unless, of course, that man should be Cole Coachman.

Both of her cousins told Marcie that Saint Valentine's Day was a day for a lady to be swept off her feet by a man, and who better to do so than a titled swell? But they also assured Marcie that should she not find Lord Sherringham pleasing, they would, without hesitation, come to Marcie's rescue. They reminded her of this fact just as quickly as they reminded Marcie that she had once written to them both, stating she wished above all other things to become a true lady.

"Come now," said the amber-eyed Meredith. "Surely a part of you wishes to be clothed in a beautiful gown and paid attention by a handsome swell."

"Please," added Mirabella, "allow Merry and me the pleasure of fussing over you. It troubles us that we were not there to help you escape that horrible boarding school Think of this as our Valentine's gift to you."

"Yes, do," enthused Meredith.

Marcie, not wanting to insult her cousins, whom she loved dearly and had long wished to emulate, finally relented.

"Very well," Marcie said, though she didn't exactly relish the thought of being primped and pampered and then sent off like a lamb to slaughter into the company of one Lord Sherringham. But who was she to dash her cousins' hopes?

And so it was that Marcie was led upstairs to a frilly bed chamber where both Mirabella and Meredith commenced to make a lady of her.

Penelope, hanging back from the commotion, allowed her goddaughters to scurry out of the room and upstairs.

Pipe clamped between white teeth, she turned to look over one shoulder, gazing beyond the curtained windows to the wintry landscape there and hoping to espy a certain Mail coach.

Penelope had been present when Lord Sherringham arrived earlier, and had—only in thought, of course—applauded the man's sense of adventure in taking on the guise of a coachman. Eccentricity was to Penelope a mark of distinction.

To Penelope's further delight, she had seen in Lord Sherringham's gray eyes the telling spark of interest when it was mentioned to him that a certain Marcelon Victoria Darlington, now an heiress in her own right, would soon be arriving.

In fact, Penelope had the distinct impression his lordship had met up with her goddaughter along the road. Why else would the man look as though he were suddenly beset with passion when Marcie's name was mentioned?

And, too, there was the matter of Marcie's becoming quite

evasive about how, exactly, she'd traveled the distance from London to Burford. Penelope had smiled to herself; the road from Town to Burford was winding, filled with surprises . . . and long enough for two people cut of the same cloth to fall in love.

Though his lordship had tried his best to appear nonchalant about coming to the ball, the wise Penelope guessed otherwise. She could see the shimmer of hope in his stormy gaze. And could perceive the presence of Cupid hovering about him. Ah, yes, she'd thought. The ball would be a glorious ending to Saint Valentine's Day. Love was indeed in the air.

Penelope had then decided she, Mirabella, and Meredith made the correct decision in dashing off an invitation to Lord Sherringham weeks ago. Thank God his sisters-in-law had managed to persuade him to make the journey to Stormhaven. Penelope had long ago guessed that the third son of her dear departed friends, the late Marquis and Marchioness of Sherringham, would be a perfect match for her own reckless goddaughter.

Both Meredith and Mirabella, however, had been most concerned when his lordship commenced to make a quick exit, explaining rather hastily that he must deliver the last of the Mail coach's parcels. Mirabella and Meredith worried that his lordship might not return in time for the ball. They also feared that Lord Sherringham might possibly have decided he wanted nothing to do with a Cit heiress and had truly taken flight so to speak.

Penelope guessed otherwise.

She grinned around the mouthpiece of her pipe. "He'll be back," she said to herself, satisfied. "He'll be back . . . or he'll rue the day he ever graced my doorstep."

So saying, Penelope blew out a puff of smoke and then

headed toward the sounds of those guests who had spent the afternoon riding into Stow and visiting the shops there and were just now returning. After she'd assured that they were all made comfortable before they headed to their rooms to make ready for the ball, she would go upstairs and check on Marcie. She had yet another goddaughter to help propel into a man's arms.

However eccentric she might be, Penelope Barrington knew the look of love when she saw it. . . .

Marcie found herself unceremoniously tossed into a tub of steaming water and then washed so hard and so thoroughly that her skin grew bright pink.

"I say," Marcie cried, "but I've never heard of a 'proper lady' being treated so roughly by her maid!"

"Then you should be thankin' yer stars I not be yer own maid, Miss Marcie," said the red-haired Annie.

Annie plunged Marcie's head down into the water, then pulled her upright as she splashed a pail of warm water over Marcie's head.

"Oww!" screeched Marcie. "That's hot!"

"La, but I never 'eard a lady scream like you can scream. And can you not be still?"

"I'll be still just as soon as you are finished. Bloody hell, Annie, but you are testing my patience."

"And you," said Annie, " 'ave the mouth of a coachman!"

Marcie didn't argue that. Indeed, she couldn't seem to get thoughts of Cole from her mind. No matter how hard she tried not to, she kept remembering the sound of Cole Coachman's voice, the feel of his touch, and the taste of his kiss.

"Devil take it," Marcie muttered, once the mobcapped

Annie hauled her out of the tub and rubbed her down with a thick towel. "I am quite capable of drying myself."

"I ne'er said you weren't. Lawks, Miss Marcie, but you 'ave the bite of a tightly coiled viper." Annie threw up her hands, backing away. " 'Ave it your way, I say!"

"I shall at that, thank you," said Marcie, and she gave the maid a smile.

Annie returned the smile with a broad grin. "I like your spunk, Miss Marcie."

Mirabella and Meredith came back into the room then, bearing boxes of chemisettes, silk gowns, and slippers.

"Where to begin?" wondered Mirabella.

"With the gown, I think," said Meredith.

Marcie forced back a groan as she was spun about, measured, spun about again, measured for a second time, and then forced into a clean and pressed chemise as well as flesh-colored stockings.

"Really," Marcie began. "You needn't go to such a fuss. I've a perfectly useful gown in my portmanteau—"

"Not no more you don't," offered Annie. The maid looked guilty, but only for a moment. "Goodness, Miss Bella," she cried, "but I couldn't allow your cousin to be seen in the likes of 'at dress! 'Twas all wrinkled and full o' rock dust. And," she added, "the cut was not at all in the mode."

"What did you do with the gown, Annie?" asked Mirabella patiently.

"I burned it."

Marcie gasped.

Mirabella and Meredith, however, strived to smother a giggle.

"Do forgive Annie," said Mirabella hastily to Marcie. "I

fear she has a penchant for taking things upon herself. I shall replace your gown. I promise."

It wasn't the lost gown Marcie was regretting, but rather the fact that she had now once and for all truly given up the life she'd known. No longer was she Argamont Darlington's wild daughter, and neither was she the most unmanageable student at Mistress Cheltenham's school. But most of all, she was no longer the mischievous miss Cole Coachman had saved from the snowy mews. All too suddenly, Marcie had been thrust into the midst of becoming a "fashionable young lady."

Marcie fought down the nostalgia threatening to overwhelm her as her cousins hurried to mold her into something she was not. There came to her ears a veritable barrage of what she should and should not do once she'd descended the stairs and joined Aunt Nellie's Saint Valentine's Day ball.

Her hair was dried and then twisted into a fetching bob of burnished coppery curls by the ever handy Annie. Too soon she was outfitted in a mouth-watering creation of the softest white silk, a color that would most assuredly draw all eyes her way. The comely gown with its long sleeves and skirt that flared and then was gathered in the back, formed tight to her curving figure. Next came a pair of white pearl-encrusted slippers.

"And now," declared Annie, "I be addin' me own present."

Marcie was forced down onto a stool as Annie, a paper packet of rouge in her hands, commenced to heighten the color of Marcie's high cheekbones and then added the merest touch of color to Marcie's pouty mouth. "There," Annie said. She smiled, pleased.

Marcie was half afraid to peer into the small mirror Annie thrust in front of her. Marcie screwed up her courage. She looked, then gasped in awe.

"That—that isn't truly me, is it?"

Both Mirabella and Meredith stepped behind her. "It is," they said in unison.

"You look lovely, Marcie," said Meredith.

"Very lovely indeed," added Mirabella.

"A true goddess!" declared Annie.

Just then, there came a loud knock upon the door of the chamber.

"My dear Bella," boomed a very male voice, "I shall view this new cousin of mine! Pray, do not keep me waiting much longer."

Mirabella smiled. "It is my husband," she explained. "Christian has been wanting to meet you, Marcie, for Aunt Nellie has piqued his interest in our mischievous cousin from the West Country. And truth to tell, I've been wanting *you* to meet *him*. You'll adore each other. You wouldn't mind if he just popped his head inside the door for a quick introduction, would you? I know it's most improper, but since we're all presentable, and since nothing is ever normal at Stormhaven, well . . ."

Marcie laughed. "Oh, just open the door, will you, Bella? I am curious about the man who finally captured the heart of the 'Unmatchable Miss Mirabella'!"

Mirabella instantly obliged.

Marcie found herself staring at the most handsome man she'd ever seen—save Cole Coachman, of course. He was tall and strapping, with a wealth of jet-black hair curling back from exquisitely lean features and presenting a stark contrast to his expertly tied, snow-white cravat.

His mouth curved into a broad smile at sight of Marcie. "Wherever have you been hiding this lovely creature, my dearest Bella?"

Marcie blushed.

Mirabella moved toward her husband. "Christian, do put your eyes back into your head lest you make a perfect cake of yourself," she teased and then went on to make introductions. It was obvious the well-traveled Mirabella, once known among the ton as the "Unmatchable Miss Mirabella" had at last found true love. Mirabella had finally given up her wandering ways once she'd met and married the darkly handsome Christian Philip Edward White, new Earl of Blackwood.

There was much laughter and merriment as Mirabella recounted to Marcie the tricky path to love and happiness she and Blackwood had taken. Mirabella and her husband exchanged private smiles while retelling a convoluted tale that involved not only a King Charles spaniel, but a dog-eating tiger named Sasha as well. It was apparent to Marcie that Blackwood and Bella were very much in love with each other.

Marcie sighed. Ah, how she, too, wished to find such happiness. She said as much to her cousins.

"Oh, but you shall," insisted the sweet Meredith.

"Indeed," added Mirabella. "In fact, I have every hope that our Lord Sherringham has returned from his . . . uh . . . business venture. Surely, he will be waiting downstairs for you. Come, Marcie, let us prepare you for your grand entrance."

Marcie appreciated her cousins' concern on her behalf, but still she did not fashion to make a perfect widgeon of herself in front of some fine swell. Nor did she wish to capture the interest of any man—save Cole Coachman. But she allowed herself to be schooled in the fine arts of a true lady nonetheless.

Marcie found herself near breaking under the strain of relearning so many of the lessons Betina Cheltenham had halfheartedly tried to teach her.

"Marcie!" scolded Meredith, when Marcie made total havoc of pretending to eat an artichoke. "You are to delicately approach an artichoke's layers, not destroy the thing."

"But I hate artichokes," said Marcie truthfully.

Unfortunately, no one was listening.

" 'Tis the left fork you use," reminded Annie when Marcie erroneously decided to make use of the inner fork at precisely the wrong moment through the pretend dinner.

To Marcie's dismay, there were more lessons.

"Stand straighter," coaxed Mirabella. "And do not, I pray, rush down the stairs! We want Lord Sherringham to be able to view you from afar, not be witness as you tumble down the stairs."

Marcie gnashed her teeth and then sought to soothe her nerves by pretending that it was into Cole's arms she was heading. She wasn't surprised when her nervousness ceased and she glided down a set of imaginary stairs.

"Perfect!" cried her cousins in unison.

Marcie snapped her eyes open. She was saddened when she didn't see her Lord Monarch materialize in front of her.

No one seemed to notice her disappointment.

"Now we must do something about that fan fluttering of yours, Marcie," said Mirabella. "Do remember that you are not putting out a fire with your fluttering, my dear! You must wave the fan gently but firmly. See?"

Mirabella demonstrated.

Marcie decided fans were for the birds. What need had she of a fan? If a room was not overly warm, then why bother to flutter the fan at all? Marcie said as much.

Mirabella and Meredith frowned. Blackwood judiciously hid a smile.

Aunt Nellie, having just arrived from downstairs, leaned against the doorjamb and sent her youngest goddaughter yet another conspiratorial wink. "Tell them you'd rather use a fan to slap the hands of an overardent suitor, my girl," she suggested. "Lord knows I've slapped a good many suitors while on the dance floor."

"Dancing!" cried Meredith. "Oh, but we'd quite forgotten about that."

Mirabella eyed Marcie. "Can you dance, Marcie?"

Marcie thought of the simple jig Jack had taught her in the stables. "A—a bit," she answered.

Mirabella and Meredith exchanged worried glances.

"I guess it will have to do," said Meredith.

"There might still be time to teach her a few steps before tonight," offered Mirabella, hopefully.

Marcie grimaced. "Perhaps I should just not attend the ball at all."

"Never that!" chorused both her cousins in unison.

Blackwood saved the moment by leaning down to whisper into Marcie's ear. "Never fear, cousin. Should you not take to the dance floor, I shall come to your rescue and claim as many dances as protocol allows. It won't much matter if you make the mistake of placing your left foot in front of your right, or vice versa. You need merely claim that I fouled your concentration."

"A perfect idea," said Mirabella.

Marcie giggled, feeling a warmness seep into her heart. She very much liked her cousin's husband. She felt protected and safe with her family around her . . . and that, she decided a moment later as she was led to the stairs, was the only reason she took the first steps that would transport her downstairs and into the company of the Marquis of Sherringham.

Marcie remembered to keep her head held high, as her cousins had instructed, and tried to *glide* rather than walk down the stairs. She fought to keep her posture erect, elegant and natural—if one could actually *do* such a thing! And she found, to her amazement, that she was quickly given a warm and effusive welcome by Aunt Nellie's numerous guests. A great fuss was made by all, and Marcie began to believe that becoming a lady wasn't such a hopeless thing after all.

But alas, she soon realized, her momentous entrance proved to be all for naught, for the marquis had not yet returned from some "business matter" he'd previously embarked upon. No matter, Marcie told herself, for stuffy the man must be if he found reason for conducting business on Saint Valentine's Day. He obviously didn't believe in Cupid, or birds singing in the trees for their chosen mates, or even in love that could come calling on such a day.

But the truth of it all was that Marcie couldn't help but think of her Cole Coachman, who was no doubt speeding along snowy roads and delivering his remaining Valentine's parcels which he'd so bravely watched over during the miles to Burford. Marcie mightily wished she was still riding upon the bench beside him, with Prinny perched atop her shoulder and a chilling wind slicing through her curls. Ah, thought she, if only she could turn back the hands of time. . . .

Marcie's thoughts were jolted back into the present when it was announced dinner was served. She found herself seated beside a young gentleman who deluged her with stories of his father's thriving shipping company. By the time the fifth and final course was served, Marcie had learned more than she wished to know of trade in the West Indies. Though the Marquis of Sherringham was not present, his sisters-in-law were. Patricia was the elder of the two. She was a tall woman with dusky curls, a patrician nose, and shrewd brown eyes that missed nothing. Laurinda, the second sister-in-law, reminded Marcie of a sparrow, for she had a soft voice, was tiny and slender, and seemed perfectly happy to allow Patricia to set the pace for her. Though both women were extremely gracious and kind to Marcie—perhaps too *kind*, Marcie thought—she couldn't help but believe that the women had been frightfully spoilt throughout their lives. No doubt the Marquis of Sherringham indulged his brothers' widows, for every sentence either lady spoke began with "I told Sherry I wished for . . ." or "Sherry, of course, agreed with me when . . ."

At long last, the dinner came to an end and everyone moved to the front drawing room where a game of choosing one of the ladies' handmade hearts commenced. It was a game thought up by none other than Aunt Nellie. The unmarried ladies had made hearts, and all were placed upon a long table at the side of the room. Each unmarried gentlemen was to choose a heart. A name was written on the back of every heart. The fun of the game was that the lady whose heart a gentleman had chosen was to be his dance partner for the final waltz . . . and, hopefully, would prove to be that gentleman's Valentine.

Marcie, having come late to her godmama's houseparty, hadn't made a heart, and, due to the fact that her cousins had been so preoccupied with teaching her the fine points of being a lady, no one had remembered she wouldn't have a heart on the table.

"Zeus and Minerva!" exclaimed Mirabella just before everyone commenced toward the tables. "But Marcie hasn't a heart."

"Even if she had made a heart, the marquis is not yet here to have a chance of plucking it from the table," added Meredith, frowning.

"I do not mind," said Marcie, hoping to lighten her cousins' moods.

"But we mind," said Meredith. "How I wish Lord Sherringham had not dashed off so quickly, and how I wish the two of you had arrived earlier in the week."

Marcie tried to soothe her cousin's agitation with a gentle smile. "Go, Merry. Who knows. You might actually meet the man of your dreams this special night."

"But what of you, Marcie? I want *you* to meet the man of your dreams."

I already have, thought Marcie, *and I call him My Lord Monarch.*

"I'll be fine," Marcie insisted, wondering if she would ever be fine again without Cole Coachman. Besides, there was no other man she wished to have her heart than Cole.

As the merriment began, Marcie slipped away and headed upstairs, where the children and their governesses were spending the evening. Marcie found herself in the midst of a crew of rambunctious children. Several governesses were shaking their heads in dismay at the children's chattering noise and hasty movements, but Marcie just laughed. She remembered clearly what it was to be young and unfettered and let loose in a place where no parents were present.

She threw herself into a hectic game of charades with the youngsters, laughing with them when no one could get the clue of a Cupid spearing a lady's heart—not even Marcie.

Soon, the band of children broke apart, some of them commencing a game of tag within the room and a few serious others sitting down for a game of chess.

Marcie gravitated toward the tag players and then, once she was worn out chasing around sofas and such after them, moved to the few children playing chess.

A tiny slip of a girl appeared at Marcie's side. The child

looked directly at her, and to Marcie the girl's large, expressive gray eyes were hauntingly familiar; they reminded Marcie of Cole Coachman.

"Hello," Marcie said, once again unnerved by thoughts of Cole. "What is your name?"

"Julie," replied the tiny wren of a girl. She held up the doll she'd been clutching to her chest. "I cannot tie Doll's new bonnet."

Marcie smiled. "Here," she said. "I'll help you." Carefully, Marcie worked the intricately made bonnet atop Doll's head, then tied a bow beneath the porcelain chin. "How's that?"

"Perfect!" Julie beamed, smiling a wide grin that held a flash of someone too dear to Marcie. "The bonnet was a gift from Uncle Sherry. He promised to teach me how to tie a pretty bow—just like the bow you made." Julie hugged Doll tight. "I love my new bonnet. Uncle Sherry knew I would. He is the Marquis of Sherringham," she whispered proudly.

Marcie stilled. "Oh?" she murmured.

Julie nodded, dark curls bobbing. "Uncle Sherry is a very *important* man," she added, clearly awestruck by her uncle.

"Indeed he is," agreed Marcie, thinking of the stuffy Marquis of Sherringham she was destined to meet. A part of her was surprised that such a man would deign to gift his niece with a new bonnet for a favored doll.

"Uncle Sherry always takes me for lemon-ice when we're in Town. My sister Penny says he is just being polite."

"But you know better," Marcie hazarded, seeing the girl's eyes light with love.

Julie nodded. "Uncle Sherry loves me," she said, utterly sure in that knowledge. "He might not always tell me so, but I know he does." She gazed down at her doll, smiling. "It is a very pretty bonnet, is it not?"

"Yes, Julie, it is."

The child then moved off, leaving Marcie to stare after her. Marcie thought of the girl's haunting gray eyes—eyes that reminded her of Cole Coachman. Cole had talked of his many nieces. Had he ever bought a bonnet for one of them? Marcie felt certain that he might have. As for the Marquis of Sherringham, she pondered over the fact that she'd heretofore thought him stuffy and unfeeling only because of his exalted title. No doubt she'd listened too often to her father telling her that all swells were stuffy folk. Perhaps Lord Sherringham would prove different. Perhaps the man would not be as high-handed as she'd imagined. She must not judge him before she'd even met him. But the trouble was, Marcie did not wish to meet him. She could not imagine that his lordship would be more intriguing, more exciting than Cole Coachman.

The sounds of the other adults moving into the ballroom downstairs could suddenly be heard. There was much gaiety. No doubt the ladies and gentlemen were looking forward to the last waltz, the ladies wondering who would be their Valentine, and the gentlemen keeping the name of their dance partner a secret. It was time to go into the ballroom. Time for dancing, and dreaming, and finding one's true Valentine . . . but not for her. Marcie felt her heart constrict.

She left the children, heading downstairs, but held back from the other adults as they streamed, coupled arm-in-arm, inside the candlelit room. She had no place in their merriment, no special other within the group whom she hoped to love and trust and honor forever. She drew away from their course, veering instead back into the room they'd just departed. She saw a ribbon of forgotten pink lace, most likely fallen from one of the many hearts that had graced the tables. Absurdly enough, her eyes teared at the sight. How she wished she'd had a heart upon the table for Cole Coachman, and that he'd been present to pluck it up and hold it close. But such a thing was not to be.

Marcie picked up the lace and moved toward one of the window seats, where one of the eligible ladies had obviously made her Valentine's heart, for there was a bit of paper, some shears, an ink pot and quill, and even a lone white ribbon.

Marcie scooped up the shears and began to cut a heart out of the pink paper, her eyes misting as she thought of Cole. She kept cutting, barely able to see past her tears, and was rewarded with a lopsided, woeful-looking heart. She cut two holes in it, one at the top, the other at the bottom, and pulled the pink lace and white ribbon through each. She then tied two bows and, dipping the quill into the ink pot, wrote the words *To My Lord Monarch* on the front, and on the back, *From your Mischievous Miss Marcie*. She then propped the heart against the window. It tipped against its lopsided edge, looking sorry and silly and as miserable as Marcie felt.

Marcie sighed, staring out into the dark, wintry night. Where was her Cole Coachman? What was he doing? Was he warm and safe, enjoying the holiday? Or was he still traveling along the winding roads of the Cotswolds, urging his team ever northward? Marcie didn't know.

She did know, however, that she missed him, his smile, his warmth, and the sight of his fog-colored eyes. Missing him would be the bane of her life . . . and remembering him, she decided, would be her only joy.

She wondered how life could be so cruel and so giving all at the same time.

* * *

Penelope found Marcie just as Marcie placed the heart against the window. After a moment of just watching her goddaughter, she said, "You look like a sad Cupid."

Marcie jerked her gaze away from the window, surprised to find her godmama in the room. "I guess I am just overly tired, Aunt Nellie."

Penelope reached for the pouch of tobacco hanging about her waist, then packed some of the weed into the bowl of her pipe. "Seems to me, my dear, you are rather a woman in love." She moved across the room, coming to stand beside her goddaughter. "Care to tell me about it?"

Marcie sat up straight. "However could you have guessed?"

Penelope smiled round the mouthpiece of her pipe. "I have traveled far and wide during my long life, and if I have learned one thing, it is that love, though it can wear many disguises, has but one spark. I see that spark in you now, my dear."

Marcie lowered her lashes. " 'Tis true," she admitted, needing to share her secret. "I have fallen in love." She lifted her gaze to her godmama. "I've fallen in love with a man who wants nothing to do with a willful miss who has run away from her boarding school. He—he is a coachman who takes much pride in his work, and who, alas, has little time for a mischievous miss such as me. I fear I am not at all what he desires," she uttered hopelessly.

Penelope's eyes narrowed. "Are you certain of this, Marcie? Are you sure the man wants nothing to do with you?"

"I am," Marcie whispered, and then she bent her head, trying not to allow her emotions to overtake her yet again.

Penelope was not fooled. She reached down to give one

of Marcie's hands a gentle squeeze. "Take heart, my dear Marcie," she whispered. "Saint Valentine's Day is a time of lovely miracles. All manner of wondrous things might occur, you know."

"Do you really think so, Auntie?"

"I do," replied Penelope. "Now dry your eyes, take a moment to compose yourself, and then join us in the ballroom." With that, she turned and headed out of the drawing room.

Marcie stayed where she was for a moment, pondering Penelope's words. Though Marcie knew in her heart she would most likely never see Cole Coachman again, she also realized that she'd been blessed by being given such loving cousins and godmama . . . and, too, there remained the possibility of one day meeting up with her handsome coachman. After all, she intended to return to the vicarage and retrieve Freddie, and Masters Neville and Theodore. Who knew what the road from Stormhaven to the vicarage might hold?

Marcie, ever hopeful, decided then and there that she should join the Valentine's celebration and set her own woes aside. So thinking, she left the window seat and headed for the ballroom to join the others.

There was much dancing and merriment. The musicians Penelope had hired played their instruments with precision. The guests danced divinely and laughed amongst themselves. And they whispered about the mystery of who would be paired with whom for the final waltz. The room was filled with love and laughter.

Marcie felt like an odd wheel. She did her best to mingle

with the crowd, and to look as though she belonged. But her thoughts remained with Cole Coachman.

Just before midnight, and before the last waltz began, Marcie slipped out through the terrace doors, glad her godmama had thought to have the groundskeeper sweep away all the snow from the stone walkway leading to the inner fountain of the frozen garden. Even the garden walks had been brushed clean.

Marcie wrapped her arms about her and moved slowly toward the inner fountain that was coated in ice. From beyond, she could hear the laughter from inside the house.

She was alone.

Or at least she'd thought she was.

All of the other guests were inside the house. All but one, that is.

He stood—rather nervously Marcie thought—just to the right of the fountain. Marcie strained to make out his features, but the bright light of the lamps strung about the wintry garden on either side cast the man's face in shadows. She thought she recognized the broad width of the shoulders, the way in which he held his head high. . . .

But no, she told herself. She was imagining things. The man wasn't Cole Coachman.

"There is punch and sweetcakes inside," Marcie offered, motioning toward the house.

The man did not move.

Marcie, though at first frightened, found she could not move from her spot. A chill wind whispered against her. The lights wavered. She heard the musicians begin to play the final waltz far off in the distance. Saint Valentine's Day was drawing to a close.

"Please," said Marcie, feeling an inexplicable and odd sort of connection to the lone man cloaked in shadows. She didn't want him to miss out on the last bit of gaiety in the ballroom. "Go inside and join the merriment. I'd hate for you to spend the final moments of Saint Valentine's Day alone."

"Why?" whispered the still figure.

Why indeed? thought Marcie. But she knew why. It was because she suddenly believed in the wonder of Saint Valentine's Day. Though she had lost Cole Coachman for now, she very much trusted that she might yet again meet him, somehow, someway, in the future. And lastly, she remained very much a mischievous miss who could not turn her back on any mystery. The man standing in the shadows was somehow a very enticing mystery.

"Because it is Saint Valentine's Day," Marcie said in answer to his question, deciding also to join the others inside. "No one should be alone on such a night. Come." She motioned toward the walkway leading to the ballroom doors.

"You are quick to welcome me into your world," he said, still not moving. "I should warn you I have, in the past, been one to avoid a crush of people."

"Perhaps this night could be the start of something new for you. I have been told that all manner of wondrous things can happen on Saint Valentine's Day."

"And do you believe such words?" asked the stranger, his voice oddly familiar.

Marcie fought not to make a connection between the man's voice and the remembered sounds of Cole Coachman's. Her ears were playing tricks on her, that was all. "I was once told," said Marcie truthfully, "that I am a dreamer."

"And are you?"

"Yes," she admitted, thinking of Cole and her hopes of one day meeting him again. "I guess I am."

"Pity," replied the stranger. He stepped forward, into the

light. "I was hoping you might be a believer . . . a believer in two people destined to meet."

Marcie gasped as the man came fully into view. "Cole!"

Cole Coachman nodded. "I am he," he admitted, "though I am also known as Lord Sherringham. Allow me to properly introduce myself. I am the Marquis of Sherringham, the same who was intended to pay court to a certain heiress—though I had no idea you were she."

Marcie couldn't believe what she was hearing. Cole Coachman was actually the Marquis of Sherringham, the very man she'd been dreading to meet? She felt her cheeks flame, recalling all the heated words she'd flung at him.

"Oh, what a fool I must seem to you." Embarrassment engulfed her. "I had thought you to be a coachman and not a lord," she gasped, recalling all the outrageous things she'd done. "I wish that I had never stopped your carriage. You must think me impertinent and disrespectful and—"

"I find that you are all that is agreeable," he said swiftly. "Please, do not be upset, and never, ever say that you wish you'd not stopped my coach. I donned the guise of Cole Coachman because I was weary of my life as it was. And then you appeared, and suddenly I was invigorated again for the first time in a very long while."

Marcie felt dazed. "I—I don't know what to say," she replied.

"Say you forgive me," he suggested softly. "Say you forgive Cole Coachman for his brusque ways."

Marcie felt her spirits soar. *Cole was here, he was real . . . and he had returned to her.* "I do forgive you," she whispered.

"And say, I pray you, that you love me as much as I love you." He lifted one gloved hand, showing that he held the lopsided heart she'd made for him. "I found this in the